Walking Sam

DEANNA LYNN SLETTEN

Walking Sam

ISBN–10: 1-941212-26-3
ISBN–13: 978-1-941212-26-4

Editor: Samantha Stroh Bailey
of Perfect Pen Communications

Cover Designer: Deborah Bradseth of Tugboat Design

Books by Deanna Lynn Sletten

Maggie's Turn

Destination Wedding

Summer of the Loon

Sara's Promise

Memories

Widow, Virgin, Whore

Kiss a Cowboy

A Kiss for Colt

Kissing Carly

Outlaw Heroes

Chapter One

Ryan Collier awoke in the darkened bedroom to the feel of warm breath hitting his face. He was lying on his side, and even though he tried to look at the clock on the nightstand, something blocked his view.

Then that something licked his face.

"Oh, Sam!" he groaned, rolling over and wiping the slobber off with the back of his hand.

He heard the happy swish of Sam's tail on the hardwood floor.

"Okay, girl. Just give me a minute," Ryan said, closing his eyes. Then the alarm clock came to life, telling him it was time to start another day.

Ryan sighed and rolled over to turn off the blaring beeping and switch on the lamp. At six a.m., it was still dark outside and the sun wouldn't show itself for at least another hour.

Sitting up, Ryan pushed his wavy brown hair out of his eyes. He was in desperate need of a haircut. His wife, Amanda, would have told him he needed a haircut weeks ago, and she would have been right. But she wasn't here to remind him anymore—she hadn't been for nearly three years.

A nudge at his other hand told him to hurry and get up. He smiled down at Sam. "Sorry, girl. I'll feed you in a minute."

Sam only smiled back.

After hitting the bathroom, Ryan walked downstairs with Sam leading the way. He went down the hall to the back door and unlatched Sam's doggie door so she could go outside, then he walked to the kitchen and turned on the light. Two orange-striped tabbies sat on the floor by their placemat, patiently awaiting their breakfast.

"Yeah, guys. Give me a second, okay?"

Ryan started the coffeemaker and then turned to feeding the cats and the dog. He scooped canned food into each of their bowls as all three animals looked up at him expectantly. Seeing Sam, he couldn't help but smile. She was always so happy and had that big silly golden retriever grin on her face.

He put Sam's bowl down on one side of the tiled floor and set down the two for the cats on their placemat. "There you go, Punkin and Spice." He no longer felt silly saying the name Punkin out loud, even though he was a grown man of thirty-eight. His wife had named all the animals and he was used to it. Just like he was used to having a female dog named Sam. Five years ago, when they'd gone to pick out a puppy from the litter of golden retrievers, Amanda had her heart set on naming the dog Sam. But it was a female puppy that had picked her, and Amanda fell in love with her instantly. "What about the name Sam?" he'd asked Amanda.

"We'll call her Samantha. Sam for short," she'd said.

All these years later, he was still explaining to people why they had a female dog named Sam.

It made him smile.

Ryan left the animals to their breakfast and walked from the kitchen through the living room to go upstairs. Passing the oak hutch, he quickly glanced at one of the many framed photos of his wife he had scattered around the house. Brushing his fingertips softly across her lovely face, he sighed, and then ran upstairs to get ready for work.

towering old oaks and maples lining the streets. Each house had a driveway and a one-stall garage in-between the next house. But Ryan didn't use the garage for his car. His wife's Mustang still sat, unused, inside theirs. He hadn't had the heart yet to either drive it, or sell it.

When he and Amanda began searching for a house, she fell in love with the neighborhood's charm. She hadn't wanted one of the new cookie-cutter style houses being built in the newer suburbs. As an interior decorator, she saw potential in the cottage house immediately. She also loved the thought of living in a neighborhood where so many people had planted roots for generations. It felt like home to her.

Ryan glanced over at the For Sale sign on the neighbor's front yard to the right. The Finleys finally gave in after living in the neighborhood for over forty years and moved to Florida full-time this past winter. They had been wonderful neighbors, kind and friendly, and Ryan missed having them next door. He hoped the house would sell soon for their sake. Hopefully, a nice family or elderly couple would move in.

Ryan slid into his car and pulled out of the driveway and onto the street. Noticing that Ruth Davis's newspaper was on her lawn, he parked in front of her house a moment, retrieved it, and then set it close to her door so she could reach it. She got along fine in her wheelchair, but he figured her morning would be better if the paper was easy to retrieve. He got back into his car and headed for the highway.

Ryan's base office was in a high-rise building in downtown Minneapolis just a short distance from the Nicollet Mall. It wasn't too far of a drive if he didn't get stuck in traffic, but he always gave himself at least a thirty-minute leeway in the morning. He'd go to the office, collect his paperwork, then head off to the first of his two appointments. He was a computer systems salesman, and he sold large systems to businesses and

Thirty minutes later, Ryan was back downstairs, dressed f work. He never wore a full-fledged suit—just dress pants, button-down shirt, and a tie—but he always looked professior and handsome. He was a little over six feet tall and he kept good shape by working out at the company gym several nights week. He'd found that staying late to work out helped make tl nights go faster so he had less time at home to think about beir alone. After ten blissful years of marriage to his soulmate, it wä difficult to come home to an empty house.

He quickly poured a mug of coffee and made toast, eating standing at the counter. He could have sat at the large island c at the dining room table in the roomy, airy kitchen, but he chos neither. He couldn't even remember the last time he'd taken th time to sit at the table. What was the point?

The sun was making its way up by the time he gathered hi coat, briefcase, and gym bag. He poured another cup of coffe into a to-go mug and snapped the lid tight.

"See you guys tonight," Ryan said aloud to the animals. The cats were already sitting on the window seat in the living room, cleaning themselves. Ryan's last glimpse of Sam was of her sitting at attention in the kitchen, watching him as he walked out the side door to the driveway.

The March air was crisp, and snow still lined the driveway where he'd pushed it aside while shoveling. In Minnesota winters dragged on, even as far south as Minneapolis. He walked to this compact SUV and slipped his things into the passenger seat. Then he stood a moment and stared out at the stillness around him. He liked the early morning in his neighborhood before everyone was fully awake and cars started making their way up and down the quiet street. He lived in an older neighborhood in South Minneapolis, about an eight-minute walk from Lake Harriet. It was a post-WWII neighborhood filled mostly with Craftsman-style homes, postage-stamp front lawns, and hospitals. Today, he was meeting with the board of a grocery store chain about a new computer register system, and in the afternoon, he'd be meeting with the president of a bank to discuss their needs. It was going to be a busy day.

* * *

Kristen Foster walked through the home with the real estate agent, carefully assessing every nook and cranny. It was nine in the morning, and this was the first house of the day. She'd spent the last two months looking for the perfect home in a quiet-yet-affordable neighborhood. So far, she was really liking this one.

"Do you know much about this neighborhood?" Kristen asked as she studied the living room.

"It's a quiet, older neighborhood," Greg Carlton said. "The Finleys lived here for over forty years and raised their family in this house. They've moved to Florida full-time now. There's a nice elderly lady next door who is in a wheelchair, and an older man, a widower, next door. You can't get much quieter than that."

Kristen liked quiet. Her work was stressful, and she wanted to come home to peaceful surroundings. She walked all around the main floor, and then headed upstairs to where the two bedrooms and a bathroom were. "Everything looks so new in here. They must have remodeled recently."

"Oh, yes, they did. Most of it was done in the past five years. The floors are the original oak, but the tile in both bathrooms is new as are the fixtures. The kitchen is completely updated. Their neighbor was an interior decorator, and she helped them fix it up for when they decided to sell."

Kristen nodded as she pushed a loose strand of auburn hair back behind her ear. She was wearing her scrubs and had her thick hair pulled up because she had to go to work at the hospital at noon. She'd squeezed in this morning's showing because the house and the price had been too good to pass up a look at.

She loved the old Craftsman-style homes. Even though the master bedroom walls slanted on each end, it was large and they had added a walk-in closet and small master bath. The dormer window was charming, and there was a large window facing the little fenced-in backyard. She glanced out that window and could see into the neighbor's backyard, too. A golden retriever was sunning itself on the small lawn. Kristen smiled. She loved dogs. *Gabbie would love a picture of this one.*

Everything about this home was charming and Kristen found herself falling in love with it quickly. Finally! She was tired of living in the cramped apartment she'd moved into after her divorce two years before. She was thirty-two years old and had a good job as a pediatric oncology nurse, so it was time she found a permanent home. She'd just been too busy working nights and weekends to actually hunt for one. Now that her work schedule had changed to a five-day workweek with weekends off, she could start picking up the pieces of her life.

They walked out the kitchen back door that led to the driveway and down to the one-stall garage. There was a row of bushes that separated her driveway from the neighbor's. An opening in the bushes showed that these neighbors had passed through to each other's homes often. They inspected the garage and the backyard. Everything looked good. As they walked back up the driveway to the house, Kristen glanced over and saw the dog squeeze through a doggie door and disappear into the house.

"Well, what do you think?" Greg asked. "Does this one suit your needs?"

Kristen glanced around the kitchen once more. She loved the homey feel of it, the big eating area with the large front windows, and the cozy living room with the brick fireplace. The large, outdoor front porch was an added bonus. She could picture herself sitting in a rocker, watching the sunset in the evening. It was perfect.

"I love it. Let's put in an offer," she said, smiling wide.

"Wonderful." Greg stood at the island and wrote up the paperwork for her to sign. Kristen walked around the house again as she waited. The living room held a built-in hutch, and the big front window had a window seat. It was all so lovely and cozy. She couldn't wait to sit in front of a fire after a long day at work and relax. And best of all, summers here would be perfect. She liked that it was only a short walk to Lake Harriet, where she could get her exercise walking by the beautiful lake.

"Just sign here," Greg said as she re-entered the kitchen.

Kristen didn't even hesitate. She knew that no matter how much she'd have to pay, this was the home for her.

Chapter Two

Ryan ran steadily on the treadmill, his eyes trained on the television on the wall playing the local nightly news. He'd been running for ten minutes and had ten more to go.

"You should come out with me tomorrow night," Jon said, walking casually on the treadmill beside Ryan. "It's time you get yourself out there. You can't spend every night exercising and every weekend home alone. It's not healthy."

Ryan snorted as he glanced over at his friend. Jonathan Miles was also a computer system salesman at his company and their desks were close to each other's. They were friends by default, but Ryan didn't mind. Although, he grew tired of Jon constantly telling him it was time to go out and enjoy life. "It's unhealthy to exercise every night?"

"You know what I mean. You can't keep spending every night alone. It'll addle your brain. You need companionship. You need female attention. You need a good drunken night out."

Ryan slid his gaze over to Jon. "Are you going to actually exercise on that machine or just stroll?"

"I'm doing fine. I don't want to wear myself out. I need to save my energy for the ladies."

Ryan laughed. Jon was forty years old and had never been married. He was self-admittedly of average height, average looking, and a little overweight, but he still thought he was a ladies' man. "I don't want to take all the women away from you, pal. You can have them all."

Jon shook his head. "What would it hurt to go out for a drink or two? We'll go to one downtown bar, have one drink, and call it a night. If a girl comes on to you, great. If not, you're free and clear to go."

Ryan slowed down to a fast walk to finish off his run. He grabbed the towel off the bar and wrapped it around his neck. "Jon, I'm not ready to go looking for women. I loved my wife. End of subject."

Jon stopped walking and stared at Ryan, his brown eyes softening. "I know you loved Amanda. Hey, I loved Amanda. She was amazing. But she's been gone for almost three years now, man. You need to start thinking about the rest of your life. I mean, don't you miss sex? Don't you miss being with a woman?"

Ryan sighed and stepped off the treadmill. He went to a bench and sat down. There were only two other people in the company's exercise room, and they were at the other end, using the weights. "Yes, Jon. I miss having a woman around. I miss companionship and closeness, and of course, sex. But I'm not looking to go running around having one-night stands. If I ever get together with a woman again, I want a relationship. A real relationship."

"How do you expect to find a woman to have a relationship with just sitting around the house with a dog? Look at you. You're too young to waste your nights away. The girls in the clubs would go crazy over you. You're the right age, you still have all your hair and teeth, and you have a great job. You'd be the catch of the day."

"All my hair and teeth? You're crazy, man. I don't want a woman who's looking for a guy just because he has good hair and teeth and a great job. I want a woman who's looking for a man to share her life with. I'm sure I won't find that in a bar."

"You'll never know unless you try. Friday night. Come on. You can do this. One drink and you can be out of there."

Ryan shook his head. Jon was wearing him down. "One drink. Tomorrow night. That's it, and then I'm going home."

Jon laughed and slapped him on the back. "See? That wasn't so hard. You just wait and see. The girls will be flocking to you. You'll have to beat them off with a stick."

Ryan rolled his eyes and headed off to the locker room. *What have I gotten myself into?*

* * *

Friday night Ryan looked around him in amazement. They were in a bar downtown that was overflowing with people, and it was only eight o'clock. He'd showered and changed into jeans and a nice shirt in the locker room at work, and he and Jon had grabbed a burger at a place on the Nicollet Mall. Then they'd walked a couple of blocks to a bar where the music was too loud and the people were packed in like sardines.

"Two gin and tonics," Jon called to the bartender as they stood there, smashed up against the bar.

Ryan assessed the crowd. When Jon had said "girls," he wasn't kidding. They all looked barely out of high school. He'd be surprised if there was a woman here over the age of twenty-five.

"Here." Jon handed him his drink. "Let's find a place to sit near the cute girls."

Ryan thought that might be impossible. There was nowhere to sit in the entire place.

They pushed and squeezed their way away from the loud music and toward the back of the room where there were overstuffed couches and chairs. Many girls recognized Jon and hollered out to him or ran their hands over him as he passed. Ryan could tell that Jon was in his element. Jon liked nothing better than being the center of attention. But for Ryan, all this commotion was the last thing on earth that he enjoyed.

They found a spot to stand near a high-top table beside the couches. A pretty blonde was already hanging on Jon and he acted like this happened every day. Maybe in Jon's world it did.

"You are definitely new here," a female voice said from beside Ryan. He turned and gazed down into thickly kohl-lined eyes that were the lightest blue he'd ever seen.

"How can you tell?" he asked, taking a step back because she was standing so close.

"You look all uptight, like this isn't your thing. Let me guess, you're newly divorced and just getting back into the dating scene."

Ryan shook his head. "No, not divorced. But yes, I'm new at this."

The girl shrugged. "Funny, I'm usually spot on." She raised her hand. "I'm Nichole."

Ryan slowly shook it. He noticed she wore several silver rings. "Hi Nichole. I'm Ryan."

"There. That wasn't so hard, was it?" She grinned up at him.

Ryan couldn't help but smile back. Nichole had on a thick coat of makeup—so much so that he couldn't tell if she was twenty or forty. Her long, straight, black hair hung down past her shoulders and there was a hot pink stripe down one side. She wore tight jeans and a black top that scooped low, but wasn't too revealing. Her heels must have given her at least four additional inches, but she was still only reached as high as his shoulder.

"So, you come here a lot?" Ryan asked. He had to lean over and practically yell in her ear because the music had elevated by several decibels.

Nichole shrugged again. "Here, there, all around. Want to dance?"

Ryan's brows raised. "Do people actually dance to this stuff?"

Nichole laughed. "Don't worry. We can dance slow." She took his hand and led him through the crushing crowd onto what appeared to be a dance floor. She stopped and stood in front of him, placing her hands on his shoulders.

It took Ryan a moment to realize she'd been serious about dancing slow. He placed his arms around her waist and they began moving to the loud, lively beat. People all around them were dancing wildly, slowly, or just standing still, crushed together. There didn't seem to be any protocol on how to dance to this song.

As they swayed to the music, Ryan had to admit that it felt good to feel a woman in his arms again. He closed his eyes and thought about his wife and how they'd danced together so perfectly. He felt Nichole move closer and rest her head on his shoulder—just like Amanda used to do. All at once, his heart constricted. This wasn't his wife. What in the hell was he doing here?

Pulling away, he saw Nichole look up at him with questioning eyes.

"I have to go," Ryan said, knowing how rude he sounded but not being able to stop himself. "I'm not ready for this."

Nichole cocked her head. "It's just a dance," she said calmly. Then she smiled and her blue eyes shined. She reached down and took his right hand, facing it palm up. "Here. This is for when you are ready." She took a pen and wrote a phone number on his hand.

Ryan blinked. Did she really do that?

"See you around, Ryan," she said, giving him a playful wink before disappearing into the crowd.

It took him a full minute to come to his senses and then he made a beeline for the front door. Once out in the crisp evening air, Ryan took a deep breath and exhaled slowly.

He pulled out his phone and texted Jon that he was leaving. Then he walked back to his office building, got into his car, and drove home.

Sam and the cats greeted him at the kitchen door when he arrived home. He fed them and made sure their water bowls were filled. Walking into the dark living room, he dropped onto the sofa and lay back, staring out the big picture window into the clear night sky. He saw the half-moon as it lit a thin silver path through the inky sky. Stars winked all around it. Sam came over and laid down on the floor beside the sofa, seemingly content to just be near Ryan. He ran his hand through her silky fur, leaving it to rest there a while.

"I just don't know how I can ever find another woman like her," he told Sam. "There is no way I can even try. Amanda was everything—beautiful, sweet, kind, hardworking, and talented. Do they even make women like that anymore?" He thought about the hot-pink strand in Nichole's hair. Amanda had soft blond hair that always looked inviting to the touch. Would she have ever even considered putting such a bizarre stripe in her hair? Probably not. Amanda had been a classic beauty in every way. But that didn't make Nichole's hair wrong, just different.

He slowly raised his right hand and looked at the phone number written there. The last time a girl had done that, he'd been in high school. It was silly. Childish. Yet, Nichole had done it so casually, with a wink, that it hadn't seemed so strange after all.

Ryan sighed and lifted himself off of the sofa. "I'm too old for this stuff, Sam," he said, evoking a small smile from her. "But it was nice to dance again, even to that atrocious music. Maybe Jon is right—maybe I need to go out more and rejoin life." He walked to the kitchen and turned off the light, then headed upstairs with Sam at his heels.

"Maybe I'll give it another try next week," he said aloud as he crawled into bed. "Who knows? There might be a woman out there looking for the same thing I am."

Sam curled up on her pillow on the floor and Punkin and Spice found their favorite spots at the foot of the bed. It wasn't long before they were all sound asleep.

* * *

Ryan got up early the next morning, bundled up, called to Sam, and then went for a brisk walk through the neighborhood. He felt guilty that he hadn't kept up with Sam's walks over the past months. She needed the exercise to keep her fit. Amanda used to walk at least three miles a day with Sam at her side. On weekends, Ryan would go with them. They'd head to Lake Harriet and walk the paths there before heading home. Winters were always more difficult to get outside, but spring through fall, his wife walked Sam like clockwork.

Unfortunately, Ryan hadn't been able to get into the habit after Amanda died.

After their walk, Ryan headed out to do the shopping and pick up dog and cat food. He put it all away when he got home, and was just about to lay down on the sofa for a nap when he remembered he should call his parents.

His mother, Marla, picked up on the second ring.

"Hi, Mom," Ryan said, sounding more upbeat than he felt. "How are you feeling?"

"I'm fine, dear," Marla said in a quiet voice. "Your father and I just came home from having coffee with a few friends. How are you, sweetie? Working hard, I suppose?"

Ryan told her about his week and the new systems account he'd acquired and that he and Sam had been out walking. He left out Friday night's adventure. He knew his mother would agree it was time for him to get out again, but she'd also adored Amanda. It was a double-edged sword.

"I'm glad all is well with you, dear. I'm going to lie down awhile. I'll let you talk to your dad now," Marla said, her voice growing weaker.

"Okay, Mom. Be sure to call me if anything changes."

"We will, dear. Here's your dad."

James came on the phone with his usual deep, cheerful voice. "Hi, son. How's it going?"

They talked a minute before Ryan got right down to the reason he'd called. "How is Mom doing, really?" he asked seriously.

James's voice lowered. "She's hanging in there. You know how strong she is. She had her weekly chemo on Tuesday, and it was rough for a few days, but now she feels better. She had a good time visiting with old friends today."

Ryan sighed. His mother had been battling cancer for three years. It had started out in the breast but then spread to other parts of her body. No sooner would the doctors think she was in the clear that a new spot appeared. The latest had hit her ovaries. She'd gone through one operation already, a mastectomy, and now a full hysterectomy. His mother had always been healthy and in good physical shape, but after three years of treatments and at the age of sixty-two, Ryan worried that her strength would soon give out.

"She never complains. How does she do it? She takes it all in stride," Ryan said.

"That's your mother," James said. "She's thankful to still be here with us, and especially that she can enjoy your sister's kids. Those two little girls keep her spirits up."

Ryan knew that was true. His sister, Stacy, had two adorable little girls, ages three and five. Since Stacy and her husband lived close to his parents, they were over there often. His mother loved children. She'd taught grade school for years and then high school English until the cancer became too much and she'd had to take an early retirement at age sixty. Two years later, she was still fighting, but he knew having family around kept her strong.

"I wish I lived closer," Ryan said. "I feel like I'm missing so much precious time."

"Son, you love your job and you do come home often. We love seeing you, but don't beat yourself up about it. We all have to continue our lives as normal. Your mother wouldn't want it any other way."

Ryan knew that was true, but he dreaded not being there in case things changed quickly. After talking a few more minutes, he finally said goodbye. He decided he needed to go home at least for a weekend soon to see everyone. He suddenly felt very alone.

Chapter Three

For the next four weeks, Ryan forced himself to go out on Friday nights with Jon even though he didn't really enjoy it. But he was becoming more comfortable talking to women—well, girls—out in the bars and dancing with them. Everyone seemed so young to him, and he didn't have much in common with most of the girls. He was living an adult life and they were all still party girls. At least it took his mind off of being alone.

The girls he met readily gave him their phone numbers after only minutes of talking to him. That completely stunned him. Didn't they know how dangerous that was? He never called any of them—he'd feel ridiculous. He kept hoping that some night, somewhere, he'd meet a woman closer to his own age who was more serious about her life. Of course, he knew that was near impossible because a woman like that wouldn't be hanging out in a bar waiting for Mr. Right.

He didn't run into Nichole again until the fourth Friday night he was out. She showed up at his table out of the blue, smiled at him, and extended her hand in an invitation to dance. This time, her dark hair had a bright blue stripe in it, and her makeup was a little less overdone. She wore a clingy, black sparkly dress and high-heeled sandals. He wondered how she didn't freeze outside with such a short dress and open shoes. It was April, and the snow was gone now, but the night temps were still chilly.

He accepted her hand and they walked out onto the crowded dance floor and once again danced slowly to a loud, head-banging song.

"So, are you comfortable yet?" she asked him, her eyes twinkling. He couldn't tell if she was teasing him or if the band's spotlights made them sparkle.

"Comfortable dancing with you?"

"Just comfortable overall. You were wound pretty tightly the last time I saw you. You look more relaxed now."

Ryan smiled. "I guess practice does make perfect. I've been out every Friday night since I last met you. I'm getting used to it."

"Were you looking for me?" she asked, her brows raised.

Ryan considered this. Had he been? Actually, he'd thought about her a few times, and wondered if he'd see her again, but that was about it. He'd long ago washed off her phone number from his hand and hadn't copied it down. He knew he wouldn't use it.

"I did wonder if I'd see you again," he replied honestly.

"So, why didn't you call?"

Ryan shrugged. "I guess I didn't know if you seriously wanted me to. We hardly knew each other."

Nichole gave him a sly grin and shook her head side-to-side very slowly. "I don't give out my number if I'm not serious. You looked like a good guy. Safe. Nice. I trust my judgement."

The song ended and Ryan led her back to his table where they ordered drinks. He was a little curious about this young woman who seemed so confident. Women he'd known when he was younger had been less brazen, less brave. Self-assurance was a trait most people gained with age. But Nichole oozed with confidence, yet without a trace of arrogance.

Her wine and his drink came. Jon was over by the bar talking with a girl who looked bored. This gave Ryan a chance to talk privately with Nichole.

"What do you do for a living?" he asked.

Nichole sipped her wine. "I work in an herbal medicine shop just a few blocks from here."

"Herbal medicine. That sounds interesting. Is that what you went to college for?"

Nichole gave a small laugh. "No, you don't really go to college for that. But I did go to college for a couple of years and I enjoyed chemistry and biology. My parents hoped I'd be a doctor or nurse practitioner someday, but that wasn't for me. But I've always been interested in natural medicines, so, that's where I work."

Her eyes slowly gazed around the room before refocusing on him. She smiled and reached up a hand, caressing it along his freshly shaven jawline. "What about you? What do you do?"

Ryan blinked, taken aback by her touch. "Um, I sell computer and register systems to big businesses," he said. "My office isn't too far from here, either."

Nichole smiled. Her pale blue eyes studied him. He felt a cool chill run up his spine. Not a bad feeling, just a strange one. Something he hadn't felt in a long time.

"Can I ask how old you are?" he blurted out before he could stop himself. Then he felt the heat of embarrassment rise up to his face.

"I'm twenty-five," she said without a moment's hesitation. "How old are you?"

Ryan sighed. "A lot older than that. Thirty-eight."

Nichole shrugged. "It's just a number. Do you want to dance again?"

Ryan only hesitated a moment. "Sure." He led her back to the dance floor.

An hour later, they were still dancing and talking at intervals. Neither of them was drinking much. He told her about his deceased wife, and that was why he'd been uncomfortable that first night out. She seemed to take it all in stride.

"That's what's different about you," she told him. "So many bitter divorced men come in here trying to prove something. You were in a happy relationship. You have a different aura because of that."

Ryan wasn't sure he had any type of aura but he was glad that he wasn't bitter.

Jon eventually came back to the table with a girl who looked three sheets to the wind. But then, Jon looked that way, too. "Hey, you found someone. Great!" he said. He put out his hand to Nichole. "I'm Jon. You're cute."

Nichole looked like she wanted to roll her eyes. "I'm Nichole. Thanks."

Jon then went into a monologue about his and Ryan's jobs and how much money they made. Ryan wanted to get out of there quickly.

"Do you want to go somewhere quieter? Maybe for a bite to eat or coffee?" he asked Nichole.

"I could use a ride home," she said. "I never drive when I go out."

Ryan thought this was both strange and smart. *What if she couldn't get a ride? Would she take a cab? The bus? Walk?* "I can do that," he said. He told Jon they were leaving, and then cringed when Jon gave him a head nod and thumbs up. "I'm taking her home," he said into Jon's ear, then turned to Nichole and followed her out of the noisy club.

Stepping out into the crisp air, Ryan took a deep, refreshing breath. He looked over at Nichole, who didn't have a jacket to wear. "Here," he said, slipping off his jacket and handing it to her. "I don't want you to get chilled."

Nichole looked at the jacket with humor in her eyes. "Quite the gentleman," she said, but she put it on.

They walked down the block, passing other couples who were darting between the different bars along the street. Ryan turned to Nichole. "Doesn't it scare you, taking the bus this late at night or walking around here alone?"

"No. I do it all the time. It's relatively safe."

"I guess so," he said. The police did patrol the area well, but still, the thought of this young woman roaming around alone at night made him cringe.

They made it to his car and he pulled out of the underground parking lot. "So, which way?" he asked.

She stared over at him. "Which way do you live?"

"Um, I thought we were taking you home."

Nichole shrugged. "I'm in no hurry. Let's go to your place for a while."

Ryan turned the car and headed for the highway. He wasn't sure what to think. *Maybe it's all innocent. Maybe she just wants to hang out.*

"What's that worried frown for?" Nichole asked, touching his arm lightly. "I thought it would be fun to see your house."

Ryan took a deep breath and let it out slowly, relaxing his face muscles. "Better?"

Nichole laughed. "Better. You look handsome when you're not frowning."

Minutes later, Ryan pulled into his narrow driveway and stopped near the kitchen door. He turned off the car and lights, and everything was still. It was past midnight, and the entire neighborhood was asleep, or so it seemed. If not for the streetlights, it would've been dark up and down the street.

He walked with Nichole up the three small steps of the cement porch and unlocked the door. Turning on the inside light as they walked inside, they were greeted by three pairs of shiny eyes staring at them.

"Whoa, what's this?" Nichole asked, taking a step back when

Sam came rushing over to greet her. The cats whined and slipped through Ryan's legs, nearly tripping him as he stepped forward to push Sam off of Nichole.

"Down Sam! Get down!" he commanded. But it was useless. Sam had always listened to Amanda, but sometimes turned a deaf ear to him.

Nichole sidestepped Sam's attempts at attention and moved over closer to the kitchen table.

"Sorry," Ryan said. "Sam loves everyone. Let me feed these guys and they'll calm down. You can sit in the living room if you like."

Nichole walked past the animals and out into the living room.

"Great job, guys," Ryan whispered as he quickly scooped canned food into their bowls.

"Would you like some wine?" he called out into the living room, hoping it would make up for being mobbed by furry creatures.

"Sure," she replied.

Ryan poured two glasses of red wine and walked out into the living room. Nichole was standing near the built-in hutch, staring at pictures of Amanda.

"Here you go. Sorry about the animals," he said again, handing her a glass.

Nichole accepted it, took a sip, and gestured toward the photos. "Your wife was very beautiful."

Ryan glanced over at them. "Thanks. She was. And she was a sweet person, too."

Nichole nodded and then drifted over toward the sofa. "You may want to put a few of those pictures away, though, if you're going to bring other women here. It might freak some of them out."

Ryan stopped mid-step behind her and frowned. *Did she really say that?* It wasn't like he'd invited her here.

"This is a cute house," she said. "Artsy, but very classy."

"Thanks," he answered, recovering from her last remark. He was about to say his wife had decorated, but he stopped himself. Talking about Amanda wasn't going to go over any better than having pictures of her all around.

Nichole turned and walked up close to Ryan. Setting down her glass, she reached up and slowly brushed her hand through his wavy hair as she gazed into his eyes. "You really are handsome," she said softly. Then she slipped her hand around the back of his neck and pulled his lips down to hers.

Ryan's heart involuntarily beat faster. Nichole touched his lips softly with hers and slowly ran her tongue along his lips. He set his glass down and slid his arms around her, pulling her closer. They kissed deeply, and Ryan's body reacted as it hadn't in three years.

Sam walked into the room, her nails clicking on the hardwood floors, and sat down next to them. Nichole slid her eyes toward the dog a moment, and then looked back up into Ryan's.

"Is the bedroom upstairs?" she asked.

Ryan swallowed hard. "Don't you want to talk a little? We barely know each other."

Nichole smiled and kissed him again. "I'll send you my bio," she teased. "And I'll friend you on Facebook, Instagram, and Snapchat." She kissed him again. "And if you really want to get to know me, you can read my blog. It's all about herbal medicine." Again, she kissed him deeply.

Ryan would have had to be dead not to feel the deep need growing inside him.

Pulling away, Nichole took his hand and led him toward the stairs. Ryan didn't resist. They walked up to the bedroom with Sam at their heels.

"Uh, maybe the dog could go elsewhere?" Nichole asked, sliding her hand down the front of his shirt.

Ryan reacted quickly. "Go on out, girl," he said, pushing Sam out the bedroom door before closing it. When he turned around, Nichole was right there. She'd already kicked off her heels and began unbuttoning his shirt. Somewhere, in the deep recesses of his mind, Ryan knew he should say no. He barely knew her. She was so much younger than he was. They had no real connection. But his body couldn't refuse. It had been too long since he'd held a woman close, and he craved it deeply. So he let his mind go blank and his body take over as he basked in the pure physical joy of warm bodies mingling together in passion.

* * *

Kristen stood at the dormer window in the master bedroom of her new home, staring out into the early morning darkness. It was six a.m. on the second Saturday in April, and she was finally moving in. She'd been anxious to start working on the house, so she came over late last night and began unpacking boxes in the kitchen. Then she'd slept on a blow-up mattress in her bedroom. Her sister, Heather, and Heather's boyfriend, Doug, were coming over today with a trailer to help her move all the larger items. She hoped Doug would bring a friend along, too, because so much of the furniture was heavy and awkward to carry.

But now, she stood there, staring at the streetlights leaving round puddles of light on the quiet street. She was so used to getting up early for work that it had been hard to sleep any later. She figured she'd work on the kitchen some more, and by the time she had most of it put away, the others would arrive.

She was about to turn away when movement caught her eye. A taxi had pulled up in front of the house next door, and Kristen watched as a young girl in a skin-tight dress and tall heels walked out of the house and slipped into the back. The girl had long, dark hair with a bright blue stripe running through it. She couldn't have been more than twenty-two or twenty-three years old.

"Old widower my foot," Kristen said aloud to the empty room. "More like a dirty old man."

She shook her head and headed down to the kitchen where she made a cup of coffee and ate one of the doughnuts she'd bought for Heather and Doug. She'd come to the house several times over the past couple of weeks, getting a feel for it and planning where she'd put her furniture when she moved in. In all those times, she'd never once seen the "widower" around. She'd seen the golden retriever often as it made its way in and out of its doggie door into the small, fenced-in backyard. She'd thought that the guy couldn't be too bad if he owned such a cute dog. But now, seeing the girl leave in the early morning hours told her more about her neighbor than she wanted to know.

"They always go younger," she complained aloud. "In this guy's case, really young."

The whole thing disgusted her.

Luckily, Kristen had met Ruth Davis who lived on the other side of her and she liked her immediately. Ruth was in a wheelchair but got around easily. Kristen hoped to get to know her better. But as for the man next door—she could care less if she ever met him.

Chapter Four

Ryan awoke slowly in his bed, the memory of last night still warm in his mind. He smiled and reached out to pull Nichole close. No one was there.

He frowned. Where could she be? He sat up and noticed that both Punkin and Spice were lying at the foot of the bed. Looking over, he saw Sam on her pillow beside the bed. She looked up at him with big, accusing eyes, obviously still upset from being closed out of the bedroom last night.

"Sorry girl," Ryan said, feeling guilty. He glanced around the room that was only lit by the slices of sunshine coming through the edges of the window blinds. Then he saw it—there was a note on the nightstand. He reached over and picked it up. In curly cursive handwriting, it read: *See you around, handsome. Call me sometime.* She'd printed her phone number below the message.

Ryan fell back on his pillows and sighed. After what they'd shared last night, he thought that she'd at least stay until morning. Sex was great, but he'd always enjoyed waking up in the morning next to his wife, holding her close. Nothing else compared to it.

"Don't girls like to cuddle anymore?" he asked aloud. Sam stood up immediately and gazed at him. Ryan grinned. "Well, I know *you* do," he told her, reaching out to pet her head. Before he'd fallen asleep, he'd had this picture in his head of him and

Nichole waking up together and maybe going out for breakfast before taking her home. He guessed it was ridiculous, thinking that. But it would have been nice.

He finally crawled out of bed and went downstairs to the kitchen to feed Sam and the cats. As he filled food bowls, he noticed commotion going on over at the Finleys' house.

"Hey, the new neighbors are moving in," he told the animals. "I hope they're nice." He'd noticed the SOLD sign out front a few weeks ago.

After placing the bowls on the floor, he grew curious and walked to the front kitchen window, staring out. There was a beat-up old truck hauling a trailer filled with furniture. Two young guys—maybe about twenty-three or twenty-four years old—were unloading the trailer. A slender, blond-haired girl about the same age was carrying the smaller boxes in, and another girl with thick, auburn hair pulled up high on her head was also hauling boxes. He noticed how her hair shone in the morning sun.

"They look young," he announced to the animals. "I hope they aren't all moving in. The last thing we need is a party house around here."

Sam came over and sat next to him, gazing out the window. Ryan looked down at her. "Is everyone younger than I am?" he complained. All Sam did was grin.

Ryan ran upstairs and showered. It looked like it was going to be a nice day outside so he figured he'd take Sam for a walk to the lake and then get some work done around the house. Maybe the ice had gone out on the lake. It would be nice to finally see open water—a sure sign that spring was finally here. He could use a positive sign about something today.

* * *

Kristen had her arms full carrying a heavy box when something big and furry came running her way and ran circles around her, almost tripping her.

"Sam! Stop it. No! Bad!" A man's frustrated voice called out and Kristen looked up as he came running to her aid.

"I'm so sorry," he said, grabbing ahold of the dog's collar and snapping a leash on it. "She never acts this way. I don't know what got into her. She took one look at you and bolted."

Kristen blinked as she focused on the man. He was tall with a head of wavy brown hair and kind brown eyes. He looked thoroughly distressed that his dog had almost tripped her.

So this must be the old widower. He doesn't look old to me.

"Oh, here. Let me take that," he said, pulling the box from her arms. Of course, this gave the dog another chance to escape his hold and she once again ran around Kristen.

"Sam! Stop!" he ordered again.

Kristen laughed. She couldn't help herself. The man looked completely at odds with himself not knowing whether to carry the box or grab the dog. "It's okay," she said after seeing his surprised face over her laughter. She bent down and pet the dog that was now sitting politely in front of her. "Hi, Sam."

Sam nuzzled her hand as if she were starved for attention.

"Um, where do you want this?" Ryan asked, looking lost.

"You can set it on the front porch," Kristen said. "Thanks."

Ryan did as instructed and Kristen followed him with Sam at her heels. He turned to her. "You must be my new neighbor. I'm Ryan Collier, and you've met Sam." He extended his hand to her.

Kristen shook it. "I'm Kristen." She bent down and pet Sam again, then looked up at Ryan curiously. "You do know your dog is a girl, right?"

Ryan stared at her a moment. She thought he actually looked cute with that confused expression on his face. Well, cute, for a dirty old man. He was tall and looked to be in good shape. He wore jeans, sneakers, and a sweater with a light jacket over it. It looked like he was about to take Sam for a walk.

"Yes, I know. That she's a girl, I mean. My wife had her heart set on a dog named Sam and then ended up picking a girl. Her name is Samantha. Sam for short," Ryan said.

Kristen smiled. She thought his wife must have had a good sense of humor. "I like it. Sam. It's a good name." Sam reached her paw up to shake, making Kristen laugh again. "Nice to meet you, Sam," she said, shaking it.

"So, are you all moving in? Or just you?" Ryan asked, gazing around at the others who were still hard at work.

"Just me. That's my sister, Heather, her boyfriend, Doug, and his friend, Jay. They're helping me move in."

"Oh. Well, that's nice," Ryan said. "Welcome to the neighborhood."

"Thanks." Kristen noticed that Ryan had a nice smile. But no matter how cute he was, or how nice, all she could picture was the girl in the tight dress leaving his house at six that morning. Ryan wasn't the old widower that the real estate agent had painted him to be, but he wasn't in his twenties, either. The fact that he dated such a young girl irked her.

"I saw your daughter leaving early this morning. She's very pretty," Kristen said, holding back a wicked grin.

Ryan's face scrunched up. "Daughter? I don't have a daughter," he said. Then realization fell across his face and he turned red.

Kristen kept a straight face, but she wanted to laugh out loud. "Oh, sorry. She was so young-looking that I thought she was your daughter."

Ryan stared at her a moment, as if debating whether or not to explain about the girl. He must have decided not to, because he took ahold of Sam's leash, which had been hanging down on the ground. "Sorry to bother you. I'm sure you have a lot to do,"

Ryan said. "We're headed out for a walk."

"Okay. Nice to meet you and Sam. I'm sure I'll be seeing you around," Kristen said lightly.

"Yeah. See you." Ryan pulled on Sam's leash and the two headed down the street.

"Was that your neighbor?" Heather asked, coming up beside Kristen. "He's dreamy. Lucky you."

Kristen shook her head. "No, not lucky me. He's just another older guy who only wants to date younger girls. You should have seen the girl leaving his place this morning. It's disgusting."

"Oh, you mean like that old guy *you've* been dating? Dr. Strangelove?"

Kristen bristled. "His name is Dr. Bradley Hemp, and he's not that old. He's a well-respected neurosurgeon and a nice man."

"He's in his fifties and you're only thirty-two. That sounds like a huge age gap to me."

"Well, it's different with me. I've already been married to a guy my own age who wouldn't grow up. It's nice dating a man who's mature and acts his age."

"Yeah, but don't you want a guy who's not going to be collecting Social Security soon?"

Kristen sighed. "He's not *that* old. And we're not even a couple. We just go out occasionally. He's a very busy man."

Heather shook her head. "Seems like such a waste. You're too young to sit around waiting on an old guy. Especially when Mr. Dreamy Eyes lives right next door. And he has a dog. You love dogs."

"Forget it, Heather. Let's get back to work."

Heather's eyes twinkled mischievously. "Maybe I'll take a go at the hot neighbor. It seems a waste for one of us not to get to know him better."

"Don't you dare. You already have Doug. Besides, you're probably too old for Ryan's taste."

"Hey. I'm only twenty-four!"

"Yep. You're too old. From what I saw, he likes his girls much younger," Kristen said.

Heather rolled her eyes and walked back to the house and Kristen followed. She turned and gazed down the street where Ryan had walked with Sam. Such a shame. He was kind of cute, and Sam was adorable. She shook off her thoughts and headed inside.

* * *

My daughter? Really? Did she really think I was old enough to have a daughter that age? Ryan stewed the entire time he and Sam walked to Lake Harriet. At first, he hadn't known if Kristen was serious about Nichole being his daughter or if she was just giving him a hard time. He didn't know her at all, so he had no way of knowing if she was teasing. And he hadn't wanted to correct her, either. *No, that was just a woman I slept with last night.* Yeah. Like that would have sounded so much better.

Ryan had been surprised when Sam bolted over to the new neighbor. It wasn't like her to do something like that. He'd always had the feeling that Sam liked women better than men—she'd been extremely attached to Amanda—but she'd never gone out of her way before to greet someone. He wondered if Sam's doggie intuition saw something in Kristen that he didn't. Sure, the new neighbor was cute. Her auburn hair was the first thing he'd noticed. It was shiny and thick. Ryan found himself wondering what it would feel like to run his fingers through it. Why would he think something like that? He never had thoughts like that. Her eyes were also pretty. They weren't blue, or green. More like a combination of both colors. She also looked to be in good shape, even though she'd been wearing a loose sweatshirt over jeans. That box she'd been carrying was heavy—even for him. He wondered what she did for a living that would keep her so fit.

Is it really any of my business? No.

By the time they got to the park, his thoughts turned back to Nichole and her spending the night. As he and Sam walked the lake path, the reality of last night hit him hard. He'd slept with another woman who wasn't his wife. The power of that statement nearly made him lurch. For ten years he'd been happily married to the most amazing woman, and he'd never given another woman so much as a glance. For the past three years, he had no desire to be with anyone but Amanda. He felt that no one could ever replace her in his heart.

But last night he'd slept with a woman—a younger woman—he barely knew.

His heart grew heavy.

He found Nichole interesting. She was different from most women he met, especially for her age. Mature, streetwise, outspoken, yet sweet in her own way. When she'd kissed him last night, his body reacted with a mind of its own. All the reasons why he shouldn't sleep with her had flown out the window. And it wasn't that he hadn't enjoyed being with her, because he had. It just seemed strange to him to hold her in his arms last night and then wake up alone this morning. He'd never been the kind of guy who pursued one-night stands. They were so impersonal. He liked getting to know a woman well, being friends before becoming lovers. That's how it had happened with Amanda back in college. He felt he knew everything about her before they made love the very first time. And it had felt amazing.

"I wish I still had her here now, Sam," he said aloud as they walked along. He glanced at Sam, who looked up at him with big, sad eyes. "I know you miss her too, don't you, girl?"

They finally turned around and headed back down the trail and then home. There was still some ice along the lakeshore, giving a bite to the breeze off the water. In a week, it would all be gone and spring would be here. Finally.

As they walked through the quiet neighborhood, Ryan thought again about Nichole. Maybe she'd left early because she had to work today. Otherwise, she might have stayed. He thought he would give her a call later to see if she wanted to go out for dinner or a movie or something. He did find her intriguing. Maybe there was something between them after all. He'd have to explore it further to find out.

When he got home, the big trailer and truck were gone from next door. He saw two cars in the driveway. He figured Kristen and her sister were inside putting things away. He stood there, staring at the house a moment. It might be fun having a new neighbor. She seemed nice enough. Maybe they'd get to know each other better as time went on.

"Come on, Sam," Ryan said as they walked through the side door into the kitchen. "Let's grab some lunch. You know the cats are always ready to eat."

* * *

Kristen spent all day Saturday putting her kitchen and bedroom in order. Heather stayed to help for a while but then had to go. She and Doug were meeting friends for dinner.

"You're more than welcome to come along," Heather told her as she got ready to leave.

"Thanks, sweetie, but I have plenty to do here. You know how much I hate messes. I'll be working on this place all night."

"Well, don't overwork yourself. I can come over tomorrow and help some more if you like."

"You don't have to. Just enjoy your Sunday. I'll be fine."

Heather left with a hug goodbye and Kristen stood in the middle of the living room, assessing her next move. She had made the kitchen and bedroom a priority because she couldn't cook in a messy kitchen or sleep in a bedroom when things weren't put away properly. She knew it was silly, but that was how she was. She liked being organized. And she only had until Monday to get her house put together before her long workweek started.

She worked the rest of the day on each room, unpacking boxes and moving furniture this way and that. Her mother's china went into the built-in hutch, and she placed a couple of family photos there, too. She wished her mother were here to see this house. She'd be so proud of her. Well, maybe a little disappointed that her marriage hadn't worked out, but still proud. But her mother had died five years ago of a heart attack that no one could have ever expected.

Her mother, for the most part, had been healthy. She'd walked every day, ate well, and kept her weight down. She smoked in her younger years, but had quit long ago, when Kristen was young. Yet still, one day her mother was fine and the next she was gone. It had been quite a blow to her and Heather, basically leaving them with no family at all. Heather had been only nineteen but was already attending college. Kristen had already received her Registered Nursing Degree, and was working at the Children's Cancer Hospital in Minneapolis by then. Their grandparents were both dead and they hadn't seen nor heard from their father since the day he walked out when Kristen was nine years old.

That's what men did. They left when things didn't go their way. At least, that was Kristen's experience.

She moved the living room furniture around until she liked the arrangement. It wasn't difficult sliding the heavy pieces on the hardwood floors. Once she was settled, Kristen planned on buying large area rugs to place near the sofa and under the dining room table. It would make the rooms feel cozier.

Around eight-thirty that evening, Kristen finally stopped unpacking and moving furniture around. It had been a long day and she was tired and hungry. She decided to heat up some of the homemade soup she made each week and kept in the fridge. Last week she'd made chicken noodle soup with thick homemade noodles and big chunks of chicken and vegetables. She'd made extra, knowing she wouldn't have time to cook any for a while. She heated up enough for a bowlful, then sliced two thick pieces of French bread. Sitting at her small kitchen table by the big window, she ate her food and watched as evening settled in around the neighborhood. The real estate agent had been right. The neighborhood was very quiet. Lights lined the streets, giving off a soft glow. With the old-style homes and the tall trees all around, it felt like being a part of a small town—very Mayberryish. After living in a noisy apartment building on a busy street, Kristen welcomed the quiet.

After eating, she went out on her front porch and sat in the wooden rocker she'd placed there. It was a cement porch surrounded by low stucco walls with pillars on either side of the entryway. A roof above gave protection from sun or rain. Lining the front wall were tall rosebushes that were just beginning to bud. Kristen couldn't wait to see what flowers bloomed around the house this spring. She wasn't much of a gardener, but she did love plants and flowers.

She leaned back in her rocker and closed her eyes, enjoying the feel of the cool air and the silence. Suddenly something wet touched her hand and she jumped and opened her eyes.

There sat Sam, smiling up at her and wagging her tail.

"You scared me half to death, girl," Kristen said, patting the dog's head. "I didn't even hear you walk up here."

"Sam! Come! Now!" Ryan's voice sliced through the still

night. He wasn't yelling, but in the silence, it echoed through the yard just the same.

"She's over here!" Kristen called out.

A minute later, Ryan walked up on the front porch. "Sam, what on earth are you doing?" He looked apologetically at Kristen. "I'm so sorry. I hope she wasn't bothering you. She never, ever runs off like that. Now twice in one day she's disturbed you."

"I don't mind," Kristen said. She pet Sam down her silky back. "She was just visiting me."

Ryan shook his head but smiled. He crossed his arms and leaned against the pillar. "Did you get all moved in?" he asked.

"As much as I can in one day. Most of the furniture is in the right rooms, I just have to move it around until I like the arrangement. What about you? Did you two have a good walk?"

"Yeah. It was beautiful today. We walked to the lake and followed the trail there, then headed home."

"How far is Lake Harriet from here?" Kristen asked.

"About an eight-minute walk, depending on how fast you are."

"That's perfect. I usually try to walk three to five miles every morning or evening, depending upon my schedule. I can't wait to explore the neighborhood."

Ryan nodded. "My wife used to walk like that every day, too. She'd take Sam with her. I haven't been able to keep up with Sam's walks like she did. I usually work out at the company gym every evening and by the time I get home, I'm too tired to do much else."

"Where do you work?"

"Carlson's Custom Computers. I sell computer and register systems to big businesses and chain stores. Hospitals, too."

"Really? Did you sell the system to Children's Cancer Hospital? We just switched over to the new system last fall and it was a pain," Kristen said, wrinkling her nose.

Ryan chuckled. "No, I didn't, but I would have loved to have sold them that system. That would have been one heck of a commission."

"I suppose so," Kristen said. She continued stroking Sam's fur as they talked. Sam laid down beside her chair and enjoyed the attention.

"What do you do at the hospital?" Ryan asked, sounding interested.

"I'm a pediatric oncology nurse. I work with children cancer patients."

"Wow. It must be hard, working around sick children. I mean, heartbreaking. It takes a very special person to do what you do. I'm impressed."

Kristen sat quietly, not sure how to respond. Ryan's tone had sounded as if he were in awe of what she did. Her ex-husband had never given her credit for the type of work she did. But this stranger had made her feel special with just a couple of sentences.

"That's kind of you to say. And yes, it can be difficult, but it's rewarding, too. The children are so amazing. They're the special ones, not me."

Ryan smiled. She thought he had the most adorable smile.

"I suppose we should leave you alone. You've had a busy day. Sorry about Sam bothering you. I'll try to keep her from running over here all the time."

"I really don't mind. I like Sam. Maybe she and I could go walking together sometime. I'd enjoy the company."

"We'll probably go walking again tomorrow. Do you want to come along? I can show you the way to the park," Ryan offered.

"Oh." Kristen hesitated. Just this morning she'd thought he was a dirty old man chasing younger women. But he seemed harmless.

"I'm sorry. I didn't mean to make you uncomfortable," Ryan said, a worried crease forming across his forehead.

"No, you didn't. I was just thinking about all I have to do. I'd like to join you two on a walk. Just knock on the door tomorrow when you're ready to go. I get up early, by habit, so I'll be ready anytime."

Ryan's face relaxed. "Okay. Great. See you tomorrow. Come on, Sam. Let's go home."

Sam slowly stood up, stretched, and then she followed Ryan down the three steps off the porch and across the lawn to their house.

Kristen watched them as they walked up onto their own front porch and then disappeared into the house. Ryan seemed like a nice guy after all. And he liked dogs, which was a plus.

Kristen yawned. She was suddenly very tired. It was time to go to bed. She stood, stretched, and headed inside her new home.

Chapter Five

Ryan awoke the next morning feeling rested and relaxed. He was happy he hadn't gone out last night after all. He'd called Nichole earlier in the afternoon to see if she'd like to go out for dinner that night, but she didn't answer. Then, a while later, he'd received a text from her saying she'd be out that evening and he should come down to the bar and join her. He'd texted back that he was staying home instead and he'd catch up with her another day. "Maybe we could go out for coffee some morning, or for lunch," he texted her. She never answered.

"I prefer talking over texting," he'd told Sam, who didn't seem to have an opinion one way or another.

The sun filtered in through the edges of his blinds, telling him it was going to be another nice day. Getting out of bed, he slipped on a T-shirt and headed down the stairs to feed the animals their breakfast. He was looking forward to walking to the lake today with Kristen. He enjoyed walking Sam, but to actually have someone to talk to would be fun for a change. For a brief second, he wondered if Nichole enjoyed going for walks. He thought she probably wouldn't, especially if it included Sam. She hadn't exactly taken to Sam or the cats the other night. But Kristen seemed to enjoy Sam's company, and that made Ryan like her even more.

It was ten o'clock by the time he showered and had breakfast.

He slipped on his sneakers and a light jacket, then snapped on Sam's leash and headed out the kitchen door. Kristen had said she got up early, so he felt safe that she'd be ready to go. He walked through the opening in the bushes between their driveways and knocked on her kitchen door. The Finleys and he and Amanda used to go back and forth between the houses through the bushes all the time, and that had left the opening in them.

"Hi," Kristen said as she opened it. "Come on in. I just have to put on my shoes."

Sam pulled at the leash to follow Kristen but Ryan held on tight so Sam wouldn't go running around the house as if she owned it.

Ryan glanced around the kitchen. He knew this house well from visiting with the Finleys over the years. Amanda had helped them update the kitchen a year before she died, and it still looked new and fresh. Kristen had placed a small, oak table by the windows where the breakfast nook was and only a toaster and coffeemaker stood on the granite countertop. A cutting board, knife, and a few bowls were in the dish drainer in the sink, and a big pan sat on the stovetop. It looked nice and neat in here but lived in.

"Is it cold outside?" Kristen hollered from the other room. "Should I bring a jacket?"

"A light jacket or a sweatshirt will do. It's a bit chilly," Ryan called back.

A minute later, Kristen came back wearing jeans, sneakers, and a light-blue sweatshirt over her long-sleeved T-shirt. Ryan noticed right away that the color of the sweatshirt brought out the blue in her eyes. Her hair was pulled up in a ponytail and her face was free of makeup. Her dark eyebrows and the lashes that framed her eyes made makeup unnecessary.

"All ready," she said with a smile.

"Looks like you've been busy this morning," Ryan said, nodding toward the dish drainer.

"Oh, yeah. I was cutting up vegetables. I'm going to make a big pot of vegetable beef soup when I get home."

"Are you having company over tonight?" Ryan asked.

Kristen shook her head. "No. I usually make a big pot of soup every weekend and store it in jars in the fridge so I have quick meals for the week. I love homemade soup."

"That sounds delicious."

"I'll bring you over a jar when I'm finished," she offered.

"Thanks. That would be nice."

They headed out the kitchen door and she locked it behind her, and then they started walking down the street. Sam stayed close to Kristen, nearly tripping her twice. "Maybe if I hold her leash she'll stay on the other side of me," she suggested. Ryan gave her the leash and soon they were walking easily down the sidewalk without any fear of Sam tripping them.

"Sam sure does like you," Ryan said, glancing over at the dog. "I've never seen her take so quickly to anyone else besides my wife, Amanda."

"I'll take that as a compliment," Kristen said. "Sam must sense how much I love dogs."

They walked along, crossing quiet streets and going up one block, then turning down another. Most of the homes in the neighborhood were older, all built post WWII. The trees in the yards and that lined the streets were mature, towering over homes.

"I just love it here," Kristen said, looking around. "Every house has character and the trees and bushes are grown up and look beautiful. It's so much nicer than those new cookie-cutter style neighborhoods going up all over these days."

"That's what my wife loved about living here. She said she didn't want to live in a house that looked exactly like everyone else's. She wanted one that was unique."

"Your wife had wonderful taste. I'm told she helped the owners decorate my house. I love everything in it. The floors, the bathroom tile, even the wall colors. She must have been a very talented decorator."

Ryan smiled. "She was excellent at what she did. I'm glad you like the way she decorated the house. I was afraid someone would buy it and change everything. She knew how to update an older home without losing its old-style charm. She was pretty amazing."

Kristen looked up at him curiously.

"What? Did I say something wrong?" Ryan asked, not sure why she was staring at him so strangely.

"No, not at all. It's just nice to hear a man talk about his wife with so much admiration. You two must have had a happy marriage."

Ryan nodded. "We did. She was my best friend."

After walking another block, they crossed the road to the park. They walked along a path until they reached the north side of the lake, and then followed another path.

"It's so beautiful here," Kristen said, glancing around.

"Haven't you ever been here before?"

"No. I've always lived north of Minneapolis, so I've never taken the time to come here. When I was looking for a house, I looked in areas close to the lake. I knew I wanted a place to go walking, and I'm glad I picked this area. This will be wonderful to walk around every day."

"That's another reason my wife loved our neighborhood. It's quiet and peaceful and she loved walking to the park."

"What about you? Do you like living in a quiet neighborhood?" Kristen asked.

"Absolutely. I love our neighborhood."

"Oh, well, that's good," Kristen said.

Ryan cocked his head. "You look like you don't believe me."

"I do? I didn't mean to. I just figured you'd enjoy being closer to the nightlife, that's all."

Ryan chuckled. "Why? Do you think I'm a party animal or something?"

Kristen shrugged. "I'm not sure what I think. I barely know you."

"I assure you, I'm not really into the party scene. Honestly, most days I feel so old that I think I should be applying for Social Security."

"You're not that old, are you?" she asked.

"No! Sheesh, not yet. I'm only thirty-eight."

Kristen smiled. "Then it'll be a while before you go into an old folks' home."

"Ha, ha."

They stopped and sat on a bench, overlooking the lake. The day was beautiful, even with the cool breeze. Chunks of ice still lingered in the lake, but it didn't stop people from enjoying the park and walking and biking the trails. Sam lay down on the ground next to the bench and watched as people passed.

"Sam sure is a good dog," Kristen said, reaching down to stroke her fur. "And pretty, too. You must brush her often."

"I try to remember to at least once a week. It helps to keep the dog fur from flying around the house. With two cats and a dog, everything seems to be covered in fur."

Kristen's brows raised. "You have two cats?"

"Yep. My wife loved animals. We were downtown one evening for dinner and a woman had two kittens left from a litter she was trying to give away. Amanda fell in love with them immediately and we were going to just take one. But the woman said she'd drop the other off at the pound if no one took it. Amanda couldn't let her do that. So we have two brothers, orange tabbies. Well, I have two now."

"What are their names?"

"Punkin and Spice."

Kristen giggled, and then covered her mouth with her hand. "Sorry. It's just funny hearing a grown man say 'Punkin.'"

Ryan smiled. "I know. But I'm used to it now. Laugh away."

"Your wife had a great sense of humor. I wish I'd known her. I think we would have been friends."

Ryan studied her a moment, a crease forming between his eyes.

"I'm sorry. Shouldn't I have said that?" Kristen asked.

Ryan shook his head. "No, not at all. I think you're right. You and Amanda might have been friends."

Kristen petted Sam while Ryan sat quietly beside her. He liked that they didn't have to fill every moment with conversation. It was nice to sit here with someone, enjoying the beauty of the park.

"Can I ask you a weird question?" Kristen said after a while.

"Sure. What?"

"Is it okay if I take a picture of Sam?"

"Uh, well, I guess so," Ryan said.

"I know it sounds strange. It's not for me. It's for a little girl who's one of our cancer patients. She loves dogs, so she puts up pictures all over her room of dogs she sees. She's been fighting cancer for five years and she's only eleven years old, so she's never been able to have a dog of her own. I try to bring her new pictures of dogs as often as I can."

Ryan's heart swelled. After seeing what his mother had been going through these past three years, he couldn't even imagine a child having to deal with all that. "Of course you can take her picture. I'd be happy to have Sam's picture on her wall."

Kristen smiled. Her eyes sparkled and for an instant, Ryan thought he'd never seen more beautiful eyes in his life.

She took out her phone and knelt down near Sam. The dog looked at her, her ears perked up, and she seemed to be smiling.

After Kristen took the picture, she laughed. "I think Sam posed for me."

"I think Sam is a ham," Ryan said, laughing along with her.

After a time, they headed home, talking mostly about the house and their jobs. Sam walked quietly beside them as naturally as if they did this every day. Ryan enjoyed talking to Kristen. She was interesting, intelligent, and had a good sense of humor. Unlike the girls he'd met in the bars, she was serious about her life and didn't flirt or act silly to get his attention. He liked that. She was just being herself.

As they walked down their block toward their homes, Ryan pulled out his phone a moment to look at the time. "This was fun. I'm starving now. Is there any chance you'd like to grab lunch somewhere?"

Kristen paused a moment, but before she could reply, they both spotted a car in front of Ryan's house. A girl with dark hair sat on the hood waving at them.

"Looks like you have company," Kristen said.

Ryan glanced up. "Oh."

The girl hopped off the hood and walked casually over to them. "Hey. I was wondering if you'd show up. You said we should do lunch, so here I am."

"Uh, hi," Ryan said, stunned. He hadn't expected Nichole to just show up. He looked over at Kristen, then back at Nichole. "We went for a walk. Nichole, this is Kristen, my new neighbor. She moved in yesterday."

Nichole nodded. "Hi."

"Nice to meet you, Nichole."

Nichole turned back at Ryan. "So, are we going to grab a bite, or what?"

Ryan glanced anxiously between Nichole and Kristen. He didn't quite know what to say. He'd just invited Kristen to lunch, but he was almost certain that she wouldn't want to go with

Nichole along.

"You two go get some lunch. I have work to do inside the house. Have a good time," Kristen said hurriedly, turning to walk away.

Ryan called after her. "Kristen?"

She turned. "What?"

"I can take Sam now," he said, grinning.

Kristen looked down, and her face turned red. "Oops. I almost stole your dog." She reached out to hand him the leash.

Ryan took it from her. "Thanks for walking with us. Maybe we can do it again sometime."

"Yeah. Sure. Sometime." Kristen turned and hurried inside her house.

* * *

When Kristen was safely inside the kitchen, she pulled off her sweatshirt and laid it over the back of a chair. The she turned to her work, making soup.

"And here I was beginning to think Ryan was a nice guy," she mumbled as she pulled out the cut-up vegetables from the refrigerator. "He already had a lunch date and he invited me anyway. I must have been his back-up plan in case she didn't show up. And I almost fell for it."

She pulled the stew beef out from the refrigerator, unwrapped it, and then started cutting it up into small chunks on the cutting board. Once that was done, she dropped the meat into a pan with a little oil to brown it before she mixed it into the big pot of broth with the vegetables and canned tomatoes. As the meat browned in the pan, Kristen walked over to the front kitchen window and glanced outside. Nichole's old car still sat at the curb. She looked out the window over her kitchen sink and saw that Ryan's car was missing from the driveway.

Going back over to the stove, she pushed the meat around in the pan. Kristen couldn't figure out why she cared one way or the other that Ryan had gone out with Nichole. *He's exactly what my first impression of him was—a dirty old man!* But after spending a couple of hours with him today, Kristen knew that wasn't true. Ryan was a pretty nice guy. When he'd talked about his wife, she'd been amazed at how much love and admiration reflected in his voice. He'd really loved his wife. It showed in his eyes every time he spoke of her.

But then there was Nichole. It made no sense at all. How could a man who'd had the love of his life already want to date a girl like Nichole? Not that there was anything wrong with her; she and he just didn't seem to fit. Nichole had looked even younger close up. Her dark hair had a stripe of hot pink running through it—a different color from yesterday morning—and she wore a thick coat of makeup on her face. She was pretty, sure, but she would have been prettier with a lot less makeup.

Kristen told herself it was none of her business. If he wanted to hang around with girls who were much younger than he was, that was his problem. She had her own life to live.

Chapter Six

Ryan felt terrible. He'd invited Kristen out to lunch and then Nichole had shown up. He had no idea she was going to come over. Kristen seemed to have been on the brink of saying yes to lunch before they both spotted Nichole. Then he saw a look cross over Kristen's face for one brief moment, but he didn't know if it was confusion or disgust. She'd given him an out, though, and told them to go on ahead. Frankly, Ryan was disappointed. He'd wanted to spend more time getting to know Kristen better.

After putting Sam in the house, he and Nichole drove off in his car to go to a little burger place downtown. It was warm enough for the rooftop to be open so they could eat outside.

They both ordered burgers, fries, and a beer. Ryan sat back, enjoying the sun on his face.

"So, why didn't you come out last night?" Nichole asked as she sipped her beer. "There was a really good band at the bar. Your friend Jon was there." She rolled her eyes.

Ryan chuckled. "I'm sure Jon is out most nights. I just wanted some quiet time at home, I guess. I'm kind of a homebody."

"That's boring," Nichole said.

Ryan smiled. "I suppose for you it would be. But you're still young. Going out is part of the fun of being young."

Nichole smiled at him mischievously. "Yeah. You're *so old*. I can't even imagine why I'm spending any time with you."

Ryan laughed.

Their food arrived and they ate as Nichole talked a little about her work day yesterday and how she hoped to eventually have her own apartment and not have to share with a roommate. "I'm so tired of her using my stuff and eating my food. And she complains that I'm a slob—which I am—but still, who cares? It would be nice to have a place of my own."

"Yeah, I'm sure it would be," Ryan said. "By the time I was your age, I was married. Sharing space with the love of your life isn't anything like having a roommate."

Nichole stared at him and frowned. "You were married at twenty-five? Why?"

"Why? Because we were in love. We'd both finished college and had jobs, so that was the next step."

"Sounds like a jail sentence. I don't plan on getting married, ever."

"Ever? Not even if you meet the right guy?"

Nichole looked over at him, her expression serious. "Marriage is just a legal way to say you have to share your belongings fifty-fifty. If I meet the right guy, I'll live with him. I don't need a contract to prove I love someone."

"True. I know a lot of people who live together and it works great. Amanda and I wanted to be married, though. It worked for us."

Nichole shrugged and continued eating.

"So, now what?" she asked when they'd both finished eating.

Ryan had no idea what to do now. It was late afternoon on a Sunday. Normally, he'd be finishing up laundry and maybe sitting down to watch some TV before bed. "We could rent a movie," he said. He and Amanda used to do that. They always had fun walking around the movie store, trying to choose. They usually ended up with two or three and lay in bed on a Saturday night and watching them back-to-back.

Nichole giggled, pulling Ryan out of his memories. "Rent a movie? Really? Where have you been the past few years? People stream movies nowadays. Don't you have Netflix or Hulu or Amazon Prime, or something like that?"

Ryan stared at her a moment. People didn't rent movies anymore? It had only been three years. "I hadn't really thought about it," he said. "I don't have any of the streaming channels."

Nichole stood up and reached for his hand. "Come on, old man. If you have a laptop, we can figure something out. We can use my Netflix account. Let's go back to your place."

Ryan took her hand and they headed back to his car. Once they were at his house, he let her use his laptop to hook up to his television in the living room and by the time he'd fed Sam and the cats, she had *Breaking Bad* streaming.

"Have you ever watched this show before?" Nichole asked.

Ryan shook his head.

"You're going to love it."

They sat on the sofa and watched four episodes of season three. Every now and then, one of the cats would jump up and try to sit between them, but Nichole pushed them back down. Sam lay on the floor beside Ryan, not even trying to get Nichole's attention. Ryan thought it was strange that Sam had liked Kristen immediately but not Nichole. But it was pretty obvious that Nichole didn't have a fondness for pets.

After the third episode had ended, Ryan stood up and stretched. "I think I have to be done for the night," he said, trying to politely hint at Nichole leaving. "I have to get up early for work tomorrow."

"It's only nine o'clock," Nichole said, shutting off the computer. "I don't have to be at work until noon tomorrow."

"Well, I have to be to work by eight. It was fun spending

time together, though. Maybe we can do it again soon."

Nichole stood and sauntered over to Ryan. She slid her hands up his chest and around his neck. "Or we can continue the fun right now," she said seductively. She stood on tiptoe and touched her lips to his.

Ryan kissed her, all the while wondering what he was doing. Did he care about Nichole? Did he want to have a relationship with her?

"What is that serious look on your face for?" Nichole asked, pulling away. "Don't you like kissing me?"

Ryan shook his head. "Kissing you isn't the problem. You're a great kisser. It's just…" he hesitated.

Nichole cocked her head. "It's just…what?"

"I'm not sure what we're doing. Is this the beginning of a relationship? We hardly know each other."

Nichole laughed. "We slept together the other night. I think we know each other pretty well. And I had fun." She traced a finger across his jawline and down his neck. "I know you had fun the other night, too. What more do we need to know?"

A delightful chill ran up Ryan's spine from Nichole's touch. His body definitely reacted to her nearness, but was that enough?

"You're overthinking it, Rye," Nichole said, taking his hand and pulling him toward the stairs. "It's just sex. We're having fun. Relax. Don't make it more than it is."

He let her lead him upstairs where they kissed again, this time more passionately. Maybe she was right. Maybe he needed to relax and stop thinking so much. He put everything else out of his mind and concentrated only on the pleasure of being with Nichole.

* * *

Kristen was up by five on Monday morning to get ready for work. The first thing she did was go downstairs and start the coffeemaker. She worked the seven-to-three shift three days a week and noon-to-nine the other two days. She didn't mind the early shifts, especially now that she lived closer to the hospital. Her drive would only be around ten minutes and she could take the side roads instead of the freeway and not have to deal with heavy traffic.

She poured her coffee and stood at the kitchen window, looking out at the quiet street. The sky was still dark, but the streetlights lit everything up nicely. Movement caught her eye, and then a woman appeared on the sidewalk next door. Kristen recognized Nichole immediately, and watched as the young woman slid into her car and drove away.

Kristen shook her head. "Guess she's a regular visitor there," she said aloud to the empty room.

It's none of your business.

Sighing, Kristen ran upstairs to shower and dress.

Once at the hospital, Kristen forgot all about her neighbor and his nightly visitor and became absorbed in her work. She worked with children up to age sixteen. Some stayed in the hospital for weeks on end, depending upon their treatments, and others came in for only a few hours a day, once or twice a week. She went from room to room, checking on each child and making sure that their needs were being met, talking with parents, and carrying out doctor's orders for diet, tests, and medication. It was difficult not to become close to many of the patients and their families. So many were here for long periods of time and she got to know them personally. She loved her job, but it was heart wrenching at times. Every day, Kristen was amazed at the strength these children had and all that they endured, yet they still kept a smile on their faces. They were heroes, each and every one of them.

At eleven o'clock, one of Kristen's favorite patients, Gabbie, came in for her weekly chemotherapy treatment. Gabbie's full name was Gabriella, but she preferred being called by her nickname. Even though Gabbie had been battling leukemia for five years, she always had a smile on her face and her big brown eyes sparkled every time she saw Kristen. Today, Kristen was ready for her with the picture of Sam on her phone.

"Hi, Gabbie," she said cheerfully as the little girl entered the hospital room with her mother. Even though her treatment only lasted four hours, the doctor always wanted Gabbie to stay overnight in case she had a negative reaction. Gabbie's immune system was fragile, so even though the treatments were necessary at this stage, she had to be watched closely.

"Hi, Kristen," Gabby said, smiling wide. "How's the new house? Have you met your neighbors yet?"

Kristen had told Gabbie all about her new house during previous sessions. "It's wonderful. I've met two of my neighbors, but there's one in particular I know you'll like. Here." Kristen pulled out her phone and showed Gabbie the picture of Sam.

"Oh, she's so pretty," Gabbie cooed, holding the phone. "Look, Mom. It's a golden retriever."

"Yes, dear. She's beautiful," Lisa said, wrapping her arm around her daughter's thin shoulders. Gabbie's mother was a small woman with short dark hair and dark brown eyes like her daughter's. Today, her eyes looked tired. She was a divorced, single mom to both Gabbie and her younger sister, Jennie, and she worked long hours at her job as a department manager at a discount store. But she always managed to be with Gabbie for her appointments.

"Her name is Samantha, but her owner calls her Sam," Kristen said. Taking back her phone, she added. "I'll email you the picture so you can print it out for your bedroom wall at home."

Gabbie smiled wide as Kristen began hooking up the IV bag for the chemo treatment. Gabbie never complained no matter what she had to do, and Kristen admired her for that. She was so mature for her young age because she'd had to grow up fast. Gabbie was small in size and thin, but she had an angelic face that drew people to her. She was smart, too, and was always curious about other people, so it wasn't unusual for her to ask the nurses what was going on in their lives outside the hospital. Some of the nurses avoided her questions, but Kristen didn't mind. It made Gabbie happy and that was all that mattered to Kristen.

"Who owns Sam?" Gabbie asked. "Is it a family?"

Gabbie was lying in bed as Kristen smoothed out her covers and plumped her pillows so she'd be comfortable.

"No, a single man owns her. His wife passed away a few years ago. He has two cats, too. Their names are Punkin and Spice."

Gabbie giggled. "That's so cute. Punkin. He must be a nice man to name a cat that."

Kristen laughed. She'd thought so too, until yesterday afternoon when Nichole showed up after he'd asked her to lunch. But Kristen wasn't going to share that tidbit with Gabbie. "His wife had named the cat Punkin, but he is a nice man."

"What's he like? Old? Young? Your age?" Gabbie asked.

Kristen's eyebrows raised. "Why?"

"Oh, no reason. It's just that he's alone and so are you. Is he cute?"

"Uh, oh," Lisa said. "Watch out, Kristen. Gabbie is playing matchmaker. She does this to me all the time."

Kristen chuckled. "He's a nice guy, Gabbie, but not my type. Better luck next time."

Lisa had to leave to go to work, but she promised Gabbie she'd be back that evening to stay with her overnight. Jennie was at her grandparents' house, so Lisa was free to stay all night.

After Lisa left, Kristen made sure Gabbie was comfortable and gave her the television remote. "I'll check in on you in a bit," she promised. "And I'll bring ice cream."

As she walked down the hallway to check on another patient, Kristen had to smile. *Is he cute?* Gabbie was so funny. There was no denying that Ryan was cute, but he wasn't interested in someone like her. She was a grown woman with responsibilities, not a party-girl. And that was fine with her. She was sort of dating Bradley anyway. The last thing she needed was to fall for the guy next door.

* * *

Ryan awoke alone again on Monday morning to Sam breathing in his face. It was six a.m., and Nichole was already gone. Ryan sighed as he got out of bed and headed to the bathroom. Last night had been nice. After his first initial surprise over Nichole just showing up yesterday afternoon, he'd enjoyed their lunch and having someone to sit and watch TV with for a change. He'd been hesitant over her spending the night, but then he'd realized that Nichole was right—he was overthinking things. Still, could he get over the fact that he would prefer a relationship with a woman to just having casual sex?

Life was so much easier when I was younger.

And maybe that was the problem. He'd always preferred a relationship to casual sex—even when he was younger. But women today were different from even ten years ago. Or at least that was his experience over the past few weeks. Of course, bars weren't the best places to look for a meaningful relationship.

Then where do you look? Match.com?

Ryan gave up overthinking *that* and got ready for work.

He had a busy Monday and didn't have a chance to talk to Jon until they were in the gym that evening.

"Wow, man. Did you get lucky on Friday night or what? That Nichole is cute and you got to tap that," Jon said as he strolled leisurely on the treadmill next to Ryan.

Ryan glared at him. "Why do you say stuff like that? I didn't *tap* anyone. And what happened between me and Nichole is not up for discussion."

Jon raised his hands in self-defense. "Whoa, calm down. Geez, guy, you sure are touchy today. Wake up on the wrong side of the bed or something?"

Ryan sighed. "No. I just don't like it when you use terms like that. It's disrespectful."

"Sorry, man, but what are you going to call a one-nighter? Making love? It's got nothing to do with love, thank goodness. If it did, I'd be running as fast as I could out the door."

Ryan glanced over at Jon. He wondered if, after years of prowling the bar scene, he'd start acting like Jon? That made him visibly shudder.

"Don't you ever want more than one-night-stands?" Ryan asked him. "Don't you want someone you can come home to at night and know that she's happy to see you? Someone to wake up with on a Sunday morning and just lie beside in bed, talking. Don't you ever want a relationship instead of picking up strange women in bars?"

Jon's eyes grew wide and he stopped walking. "Are you crazy? Why do you think I go to bars to pick up girls? Relationships are deadly. Sure, they start out fine, but then you end up hating each other. No, thank you."

Ryan gave up and started running faster. If he could find someone to have even half the relationship he'd had with Amanda, he'd grab onto her and never let go.

Chapter Seven

The days went by quickly and Ryan was actually disappointed that he hadn't seen Kristen around all week. He realized they had different schedules, so bumping into each other wasn't going to happen, but he hoped they would. He had no idea why he felt that way. After all, he barely knew her. But he'd enjoyed the short time they'd spent together last Saturday. She was easy to be around.

Then there was Nichole.

He'd tried connecting with Nichole a couple of times during the week to ask her if she'd like to go out to dinner, but she never called or texted him back. He'd thought that was strange, and yet he was relieved, too. Of course, that made him feel guilty. The whole thing felt strange to him. He wasn't used to his life being so complicated.

Saturday morning, he walked out to the small building in the backyard that his wife had used as an office. Opening the door, he stepped inside with Sam at his heels, closed his eyes, and inhaled deeply. There was still the lingering scent of her, the soft, sweet perfume she used to wear along with the smell of the hand cream she rubbed on often.

"Soft hands, warm heart," she'd tease him every time she put some on her hands.

"Isn't that supposed to be cold hands, warm heart?" He'd

tease. She'd come up to him, softly caressing her hands on his face. "Do my hands feel cold to you?"

He remembered it like it was yesterday.

Sighing, Ryan walked around the small space, touching fabric samples, paint chips, and open catalogs of bathroom fixtures. Her computer still sat on her desk, its blank screen staring at him. He hadn't moved a thing in here since her sudden death—he just didn't have the heart to. He knew he should clear it all out and put the space to good use, but he couldn't. Being able to come in here and still feel her presence calmed him. And at times like these, he needed to feel her.

Something wet touched his hand and Ryan looked down to see Sam sitting down beside him, looking up with sad eyes.

"You feel her here too, don't you, girl? Her scent, her spirit. It's still in this room."

Sam didn't answer, but Ryan saw it in her eyes. Sam missed Amanda as much as he did—maybe even more because she didn't understand why Amanda was gone.

Taking one last deep breath, Ryan led Sam outside and closed the door behind them. It was ten in the morning, the sun was shining, and it promised to be a beautiful day.

"Let's go for a walk," Ryan said, patting Sam's head.

Sam turned her gaze toward the house next door.

Ryan laughed. "You read my mind. Let's ask Kristen to come along."

He knocked on Kristen's kitchen door a few minutes later and she answered it wearing a cook's apron.

"Hi," she said, smiling brightly. "What's up?"

"Hi. Sam and I are heading out for a walk. We wondered if you'd like to join us."

Kristen looked first at Ryan, then Sam, and then Ryan again. "We? Sam actually told you she'd like to invite me along?"

Ryan chuckled. "I know. I've been talking to animals too

long. But I swear, it was as if she said it out loud."

Kristen laughed. "Sure, I'd love to. Just give me a minute to pick up my mess. Come on in."

Ryan followed her inside with Sam right behind him. "Wow, you've been busy again. What are you cooking today?"

"Split pea and ham soup."

"Smells delicious."

"Thanks. I just have to pour it into jars to cool, and then I'll be ready to go."

Ryan watched as she put a kitchen funnel into a Ball canning jar and then ladle the soup into it. She did this with five large jars and set the pan in the sink to run water into it.

"I'll be ready in a minute," she said, heading out of the room. She returned with a sweatshirt pulled over her T-shirt and jeans and wearing her sneakers. Kneeling down, she rubbed Sam behind the ears. "You were a big hit with Gabbie this week," she said. "She thought you were beautiful."

"Is Gabbie the cancer patient you were talking about last week?" Ryan asked.

Kristen nodded. "Yes. She's such a sweetie. And she adored Sam."

"I'm glad Sam made her happy," Ryan said, his expression turning serious. "Well, shall we go?"

They headed out down the street, both waving at Ruth who was sitting on her porch in her wheelchair. She waved back and smiled, and they continued on.

"Ruth is such a nice lady," Kristen said. "I brought her some of my soup last week and she was so sweet about it." She gave Ryan a sideways glance. "And she mentioned that someone in the neighborhood always makes sure her morning paper is on her porch. Hmmm. I wonder who that is."

Ryan shrugged. "Maybe the paperboy has a good aim."

"Yeah. I'm sure that's what it is."

Ryan grinned.

They walked along. Kristen was holding Sam's leash again and the dog was behaving extremely well. When they got to the park, they turned right onto the trail that headed north and kept walking.

"Is something wrong?" Kristen finally asked. "You've been so quiet."

Ryan shook his head. "No. I was just thinking about how difficult it must be for a child to have to deal with cancer. And how hard it is on the parents, too."

"You'd be amazed at how resilient children can be. Sometimes, it's the hardest on the parents. But yes, I'm always in awe of how much children can cope with. I doubt I'd be half as strong as they are if I were the one with cancer."

Ryan looked over at Kristen. "My mother has been battling cancer for three years now."

Kristen stopped walking, her blue-green eyes looking up at him with honest concern. "I'm so sorry, Ryan. How is she doing?"

Ryan stopped too, and two bikes whizzed past them as if they weren't even there. He'd never talked to anyone except family about his mother's illness. He had no idea why he'd blurted it out to Kristen. But now that he had, he suddenly felt as if a weight had been taken off his shoulders.

"She's weak, but strong in spirit. She just went through a second operation and is now doing chemo again, and I know it's been rough on her. But she never complains. I don't know how she does it."

Kristen reached up and placed her hand on his arm. He'd pulled up his sweatshirt sleeves to his elbows and her hand felt warm on his bare skin. "I'm sure your mom is a strong woman. It sounds like she's determined to get better, and believe me, a positive attitude is as potent as any medicine. It will help her get through this tough time."

Ryan met her gaze and saw warmth in her eyes. *She must be an amazing nurse,* he thought. "Thank you, Kristen."

They continued walking and then sat on a bench for a few minutes, enjoying the view of the lake. The water was still today, reflecting the white, puffy clouds in the sky.

"You know, I've never talked to anyone other than family about my mother's cancer before. It's actually a relief to finally talk about it," Ryan said.

"I'm glad you could tell me. Do your parents live nearby?"

"No, they live in Iowa. Cedar Rapids. That's where I grew up."

"Really? I just assumed you grew up in Minnesota. Do you get to see them often?"

"I try. But it's not always easy to get away from work. I need to get down there very soon and see my mom. I worry about her."

"I'm sure she'd enjoy a visit from you." They sat there a few minutes before Kristen said, "Your family has had a rough time these past few years. First, your wife passed away, and then your mother's cancer. I'm sorry, Ryan. Sometimes life just doesn't give us a break."

Ryan turned to her, surprised at what she'd just said. He'd often thought the same thing, but tried not to feel sorry for himself. He must have looked shocked, because she stared at him strangely.

"Did I say the wrong thing?" she asked. "I'm so sorry. I sometimes say what I'm thinking and I mean well, but it comes out wrong."

"No, not at all. I was just surprised, that's all. I've thought the same way too, sometimes, how these two tragedies hit our family at once and how unfair it is. But then I have to remind myself that bad things happen to other people, too. I try not to feel sorry for myself, but it's hard."

Kristen nodded. "I know how you feel. When my husband and I divorced, I felt like I was the only one with bad luck. But then I went to work every day and saw the sick children, and I'm thankful that I have my health, a good job, and I don't live with that lying bastard anymore."

Ryan stared at her, and then broke out laughing. "You do just say what you're thinking."

Kristen giggled. "Sorry, but it's true. I won't bore you with the insane details, but I've been so much happier since I moved into my own house. It's a fresh start, and I'm excited about it."

"I'm happy you moved in, too. And it goes without saying that Sam adores you."

Kristen bent down and pet Sam. "I like Sam, too."

They started walking home then, keeping the conversation flowing about their favorite music, television shows, and other topics. When they got to Kristen's house, she turned to Ryan. "Can I ask you a favor?"

"Sure. What?"

"I know you don't know me that well, but I'm going to ask anyway. I go walking every day either before or after work, and I was wondering if you'd let me take Sam along on my walks. You don't have to feel bad if you say no, but I'd really love it if I could have Sam for company."

Ryan didn't even have to think about it. He didn't know why, but he trusted Kristen completely. "I think that's a great idea. She really needs the exercise and then I won't feel guilty over her being stuck at home all day."

"So, you trust me with her?"

"Of course," Ryan said. "I can tell you like her. And she likes you, too. It's a great idea. How should we do this? Should I give you a key so you can get her?"

"Oh, no. I wouldn't expect you to give me a key to your house. I can just get her from the back yard. Do you think she'll come outside if I call her?"

Ryan looked down at Sam, who'd been moving her head back and forth, following the conversation. Sometimes he swore Sam understood everything that was being said. "I'm sure she will. Here." He unsnapped her leash and handed it to Kristen. "You can keep this one. I have another. I'm glad you'll be walking Sam. She's going to love it."

He also gave her a key to the lock on the gate so she could get into the backyard. When they parted to go inside their own homes, he was actually sorry. He'd really enjoyed spending time with Kristen.

* * *

Kristen loved taking Sam along on her daily walks. All the next week, she went into the yard either early in the morning before her noon shift or late in the afternoon when she'd get home and call for Sam. The dog came bounding out the doggie door, eager to go with her. They'd walk along, having long conversations about Kristen's day or her patients at work. Kristen knew she was safe telling Sam anything, because the dog was good at keeping secrets. She also knew it was silly talking to Sam on her walks, but it made her happy.

One rainy day, Kristen got Sam anyway to spend time with her in the house. She enjoyed Sam's company. Kristen thought she should get a dog of her own, but she was so in love with Sam, she really didn't want to. Was it strange falling in love with someone else's dog? Probably. But she couldn't help it. Sam was the perfect best friend. Always attentive, never judgmental, and a good secret keeper. Who could ask for anything more?

* * *

Ryan sat at the Bowflex machine, slowly working his arm muscles. It had been two weeks since he last walked with Kristen, but he saw her occasionally in her yard or driveway as she was coming home or leaving. She'd smile and wave, then be gone. He tried knocking on her door a couple of times, but she wasn't home. Last Sunday, she'd brought him over a jar of the homemade chicken noodle soup she'd just made but couldn't stay. She said she was off to meet her sister for lunch. He hoped she'd want to go walking, or that he could invite her to dinner, but she had other plans.

He'd also tried calling Nichole a couple more times over the past two weeks, but she never called back. He thought that was strange, but then, maybe she'd moved on to someone else. In a way, he was relieved. She was too young for him anyway. But they did have some sort of connection and he would have liked to at least be friends.

Jon came over with a towel around his neck, although he rarely sweat with the easy workouts he did. "Hey Ryan. How's it going? It's been so insane at work, I haven't seen you most of the week."

"It's going fine. It's been a crazy week, but a good one. I finally sold that large computer system to the bank chain. I've been working with them for almost six months."

"That's great. That commission should pad your pockets for a while."

Ryan nodded. He continued working his arms as Jon sat down on a bench beside him.

"You haven't been out the past couple of weeks," Jon noted. "You and Nichole must be hot and heavy."

Ryan rolled his eyes. "No, we aren't. In fact, I haven't seen Nichole for a couple of weeks. I've been staying home. Finding true love in a bar on weekends isn't for me."

Jon laughed. "True love. You're funny. I have a favor to ask of you. I've actually been seeing a woman for the past couple of weeks and she asked me if I knew of anyone for her older sister. I thought maybe you'd like to join us for dinner and dancing afterward this Saturday night."

Ryan stopped working out and stared at Jon. "You want me to go on a blind date? With you? No, thank you."

"No, no, it isn't like you think. Her sister is actually good looking. She showed me a picture of her. And she's closer to your age. That's what you're looking for, right? Someone more mature and serious? This might be the woman for you."

"I don't know, Jon. A blind date? I'm not in college anymore."

"Come on, Ryan. It's not like you're having exciting Saturday nights anyway. It's just dinner and maybe dancing. If you both hate each other, you can skip out after dinner. You'll be doing me a big favor. I want to impress this girl, and finding a date for her sister might do that."

"*You* want to impress a girl? Well, that's different. She must be special."

Jon shrugged. "I'm not getting married anytime soon, but she is sort of special. You know me, one night stands are more my style, but this girl is more than that. So, will you do me this favor? I'll owe you."

Ryan laughed. "Fine. I'll do it this one time. Who knows, maybe we'll get along."

Jon slapped him on the back. "Great. I'll text you the time and place. I'll be picking up the women and we'll meet at the restaurant. We'll have a good time."

As Jon walked away, Ryan already regretted saying yes. *A good time. Right.* He much preferred a Saturday night in front of the television than going on a blind date. Or a walk in the park with Kristen.

Yikes, where did that come from?

He knew it was true. He did like Kristen, but he was sure she had no interest in him. She loved his dog—that was it. As he showered and changed in the locker room, he hoped he wasn't going to regret saying yes to Saturday night.

Chapter Eight

Saturday night found Kristen standing in front of her full-length mirror in her bedroom, gazing at herself one last time. Tonight was one of the hospital's biggest fundraisers of the year—the Spring Fling Dinner and Ball—and she'd just finished dressing for it. Everything had to be perfect. Some of the most influential people in Minneapolis and St. Paul attended the ball, like the governor and mayors of each city. The tickets were extremely expensive, but Bradley attended every year and had invited her as his date. She was thrilled to go, and just a little bit nervous. Would she fit in with all the rich and famous people? Would she be dressed nice enough? She rarely thought about how others saw her, but tonight she wanted Bradley to feel proud to have her by his side.

Looking at her dress, she spun around slowly and watched as the full-length skirt swirled around her. Her sister had helped her pick out the gown, and Kristen had to admit it was perfect for her. It was a strapless, emerald-green satin with just a hint of sparkle from rhinestones trailing from her waist to the hem. The color of the dress turned her eyes a deep green, and the makeup applied by the expert at the salon helped to enhance her eyes. Her hair had been pulled up and styled into a loose chignon with soft tendrils falling around her face. Her heels and small handbag were silver and the only jewelry she wore were small diamond studs and a delicate white-gold chain necklace that had once belonged to her mother.

She took a cleansing breath. *Well, it's the best I can do.*

There was a soft knock on her front door and she knew it was Bradley. Carefully, she walked down the stairs, unused to wearing heels. It was only five o'clock, but he was picking her up early so they could join a group of his friends for cocktails before the dinner. All of Bradley's friends were doctors and they were much older than Kristen was. Their wives were also older and all had equally successful careers or were very active in volunteering. Even though they were always very kind to her, Kristen never felt like she fit in with his group of friends. She hoped that as time went by, she would feel more like she belonged than an outsider.

Kristen opened the front door and was about to greet Bradley when she stopped short. Ryan was standing on her front porch, staring at her, his eyes wide.

"Oh, you're going out," he said. "I'm sorry. I didn't mean to interrupt you." He glanced around, as if looking for someone.

"You're not interrupting anything," Kristen said. "I'm still waiting for someone. Come on in."

Ryan stared at her strangely but shook his head. "No, no. It's obvious you're on your way out. I just stopped by to say hi. I haven't seen you in a while. Anyway, I'd better be going." He turned but hesitated when a black BMW sedan pull up and parked right in front of Kristen's house. A tall man with wavy silver hair wearing a black tux stepped out of the car and walked purposefully toward them, a bouquet of roses in his hand. Kristen thought he looked like a Hollywood movie star coming to sweep her off her feet.

Bradley nodded to Ryan as he walked past him and dropped a soft kiss on Kristen's cheek. "You look lovely, dear," he said, handing her the roses. "I saw these and thought of you. Sweet and beautiful."

Kristen smiled. Bradley was always so kind. They didn't spend a lot of time together because of his demanding work schedule, but when they did, he was always kind and attentive.

She looked up and remembered that Ryan was still standing on the porch. Before she could introduce them, Bradley held out his hand to Ryan.

"Hello. I'm Bradley. I don't believe we've met."

Kristen watched as another strange look crossed Ryan's face, and then his eyes lit up and he smiled wide. "Oh, it's so nice to meet you," he said, shaking his hand. "I'm Ryan. I live next door. You must be Kristen's father. How nice it is that you're going out together."

Kristen's mouth dropped open and her eyes grew wide. *Her father? He thinks Bradley is her father?* Then she noticed a teasing glint in Ryan's eyes.

"No, I'm not her father," Bradley said, politely. "I'm her date. We're going to a hospital fundraiser tonight."

Ryan looked like he feigned surprise. "I'm so sorry. It was an honest mistake. Well, you two have a wonderful time. Nice to meet you, Bradley. I'll see you later, Kristen." He turned and walked away before Kristen could say anything.

"Funny guy," Bradley said, not even fazed at being mistaken for her father. Kristen nodded and went inside to put the roses in a vase and find her wrap. As Kristen stepped into Bradley's BMW, she glanced over at Ryan's house. His car was gone. The next time she saw him, she was going to give him hell.

* * *

Ryan chuckled to himself as he entered his home and went upstairs to change for his date. He knew when he'd called Bradley her father that it was mean, but he couldn't stop himself. It was the perfect opportunity to get back at Kristen. *That's what she gets for calling Nichole my daughter.* Besides, the guy was old—way older than Ryan was. So, it was okay for her to date an older man but not for him to date younger women? That was quite a double standard.

He had to admit, the moment Kristen opened the door and stood there looking like a princess out of a fairy tale, he'd been tongue-tied for a second. He was used to seeing her in T-shirts, sweatshirts, and jeans, clothes that didn't necessarily flatter her figure. But this dress had accentuated every curve and it took his breath away. Her eyes had turned a deep green and her auburn hair gleamed in the light. Everything about her made his heart skip a beat, and he'd felt a tinge of jealousy that he wasn't the man taking her to a fancy ball.

Okay, so that may have prompted his snide remark more than getting even with her. Truth be told, he had no reason to be mean to her. After all, she'd been nothing but nice to him. Well, except for the daughter remark. But when he saw the older man come up the walk, he'd reacted like a jealous fool.

Why?

As he drove to the restaurant on the Nicolette Mall to meet Jon and the women, the thought of Kristen dating that man continued to gnaw at him. Why would she date someone so much older than she was? Money? From the look of his car, it was obvious the guy was very comfortable financially. But Ryan didn't believe that was it. Kristen didn't seem like the type of woman to chase money. The guy was good-looking, for his age. And he was probably smart. That would appeal to Kristen.

Hey, bud. It's none of your business.

Ryan chased his thoughts away. They weren't getting him anywhere anyway.

He met up with Jon and the two women at a nice restaurant. As he approached the table, he noticed that both women were pretty. One was blond and the other brunette. He couldn't tell their ages, but he was relieved that they didn't look like they were still in high school.

"Ah, there he is. I knew he wouldn't stand us up," Jon said, gesturing toward Ryan.

Ryan stopped beside the booth and smiled. "Sorry I'm late. I had a hard time finding a parking space."

"You're fine. We just got here ourselves," Jon said jovially. "Sit. Let's get this party started."

Ryan stared at Jon a moment and noticed his face was flushed and his pupils were dilated. There was a gin and tonic sitting in front of him. It looked to Ryan as if Jon had already had one too many.

Ryan slid into the booth next to the brunette. Her hair was cut short but waved softly around her oval face and she had warm brown eyes. She gave him a small smile.

"Hi, I'm Ryan," he said.

"I'm Christy. It's nice to meet you."

"Nice to meet you, too." He smiled back.

"This is her sister, Alicia," Jon piped up.

"Hi, Ryan," Alicia said.

Ryan said hello, and then Jon waved over the waitress to order another round of drinks.

"Jon told us that you two work for the same firm," Christy said after the waitress had brought drinks and menus.

Ryan nodded. "Yes, we do. We've known each other for quite a while. What about you? What do you do?"

"I'm an office manager at an accounting firm," Christy said. "I majored in accounting in college, but I enjoy management much better than moving numbers around."

"Sounds interesting," Ryan said.

"Ryan's our best salesman," Jon said loudly. "He just made a big sale to a large bank chain this past week. You wouldn't believe the commission he made off of it."

Ryan felt his face heat up. He hated when Jon bragged about money, and he could tell it embarrassed Christy, too. She looked down at her menu, ignoring Jon.

"It was a nice sale," Ryan said, leaving it at that. He quickly changed the subject. "Alicia, what do you do?"

Alicia smiled wide as she turned toward Ryan. She had long blond hair and blue eyes the shade of sapphires. He couldn't tell how tall she was sitting down, but she was slender and looked nice in the blue-green dress she wore. The dress reminded Ryan of Kristen's eyes.

Where did that come from?

"I work as a receptionist at a dental office." She giggled. "Not exactly glamourous, but it pays the bills."

Ryan nodded. She was a pretty girl. He could see why Jon was so enamored with her.

They all ordered their food and made light conversation. Jon was getting too loud too early, but Alicia didn't seem to notice or mind. She kept up with him drink for drink, and she continued to giggle and hang on every word Jon said.

"Jon says you were married for several years," Christy said quietly as they ate their salads. "And that your wife passed away. I'm sorry."

Ryan was surprised that she'd brought it up but also relieved at her directness. "Yes. Amanda and I were married for ten years before she died. We had a great marriage."

"That's nice to hear," Christy said sincerely. "Not everyone can say they had a great marriage."

"Since we're being frank, Jon said you were divorced," Ryan said gently.

Christy nodded. "Yes. Life doesn't always turn out the way you plan, as you well know. But I still have hope that Mr. Right is somewhere out there."

Ryan smiled. At least she believed in finding Mr. Right,

which was more than Nichole believed in.

As they ate dinner, Ryan spent most of the time talking to Christy. He learned that she lived in an apartment about ten minutes from his home and that she enjoyed cooking and took yoga classes twice a week. She had an easy-going way about her which made Ryan feel comfortable. But as the evening progressed, Jon grew louder and Alicia joined in on the noise with her giggling. Ryan noticed Christy wince a couple of times at something Jon said, and he understood completely. Jon could be embarrassing.

"Hey, let's go dancing," Jon said after dinner was over and the check had been paid. The group left the restaurant and walked down the street to a club where the music was already playing so loudly that it vibrated out into the night.

"Here's a good place," Jon said, going inside with Alicia by his side.

Ryan sighed, and then realized he'd done so and looked over at Christy. She laughed.

"I know exactly how you feel," she said. "Maybe we can leave after a few minutes."

This brought a smile to Ryan's lips and he offered his arm to Christy. She wrapped her own around his and they walked inside, following the other two to a table.

The place was packed and they were lucky to get a small table in the back corner. Jon and Ryan went to get drinks at the bar.

"So, how do you like her?" Jon yelled over the music. "She's nice, right?"

Ryan nodded. "She seems to be."

"And Alicia's hot, isn't she? I told you this would work out. Christy's perfect for you."

Ryan had no idea if she was perfect for him—he'd just met her. But she seemed nice and he thought she was a welcome change from the younger girls he'd talked to over the past few weeks.

They'd no sooner sat down than Jon took Alicia's hand and led her to the dance floor. Ryan noticed that Christy's eyes followed them.

"Would you like to dance?" he asked, trying to be polite. In truth, he really had no desire to fight the other couples for space on the crowded floor.

"Heavens no," Christy said, then her eyes widened and she broke out laughing. "Sorry. Sometimes I'm too blunt for my own good."

Ryan laughed too. He bent down to speak in her ear. "Don't worry. I'm glad you said no. This music is too loud and the dance floor is too crowded."

Christy nodded her agreement.

As Ryan pulled away, he noticed the soft, sweet scent of Christy's perfume. It smelled very feminine. He'd missed the sweet smell of a woman these past few years.

Christy leaned toward Ryan. "Your friend Jon sure is a live wire," she said. "He likes to have fun."

"Yes, he does. How did he and Alicia meet?"

"At a bar, of course," Christy said, rolling her eyes. "I'm afraid my sister is quite the party-girl."

"And you're not?" Ryan teased.

Christy laughed. "I have a feeling I'm about as wild as you are."

Jon and Alicia came back to the table, hanging all over each other. When they started kissing right there in front of them, Ryan could tell that Christy had had enough.

"Would you like to go somewhere quiet?" he asked Christy. "We could go for coffee somewhere."

"To tell the truth, I'd really like to go home. It's been a long day."

"I can drive you," he offered.

She nodded and he tapped Jon on the shoulder to get his

attention. "I'm taking Christy home!" he yelled over the music.

Jon stared at him in surprise, then smiled wide and gave him the thumbs up. "Good for you!"

"It's not like that," Ryan tried explaining but gave up. He said goodbye to Alicia and he and Christy headed out of the club.

Once outside, Christy let out a huge sigh. "Do you hear that?"

"What?"

"The quiet. Isn't it wonderful?"

Ryan chuckled and they walked to his car. She gave him directions to her place and he drove there. "Are you sure you don't want to go somewhere and talk?" he asked. He'd enjoyed talking with her at dinner and wouldn't have minded getting to know her better.

"That's sweet of you to ask, but I really am tired. Can I get a raincheck?"

"Sure." He parked in front of her apartment complex and got out to open her door.

"Wow. An old-fashioned gentleman," she said. "Thanks."

"I know. I can't help it. It's just something I've always done."

"Don't apologize. It's refreshing."

"I'll walk you to your door," Ryan said.

Christy smiled. "That would be nice."

Once there, Christy turned to him. "Thanks for driving me home and for being such good company tonight. Honestly, when Alicia suggested this, I was hesitant. But now I'm glad I went."

"Me, too," Ryan said. "I had a good time. Maybe we could get together again sometime."

"I'd like that. Here." She reached into her small bag and pulled out a business card and a pen and wrote something on the back of it. "That's my cell number."

Ryan took it and slipped it into his pocket.

They stood there a moment, staring at each other. A cool

breeze brushed past them and the large bushes beside her door rustled softly. Ryan bent down and kissed her softly on the cheek, before backing away. "Goodnight."

"Goodnight," Christy said. Then she walked inside her apartment and gently closed the door.

Chapter Nine

Sam, Punkin, and Spice were waiting for Ryan at the kitchen door when he walked inside around midnight. He patted each of them and then slipped off his jacket and shoes. He poured himself a glass of water and leaned against the counter, thinking about the night.

Ryan liked Christy. She had a pretty face and nice eyes. He enjoyed her company and she seemed down-to-earth and had a good sense of humor. He also liked that she hadn't invited him into her apartment on the first date. It was refreshing. And when he'd kissed her on the cheek goodnight, it felt right. Like a first date should feel.

But was there magic?

He hadn't felt that strange flutter in his stomach or a delightful tingling down his spine when he kissed her. But should he expect to feel that way with anyone? He'd already experienced magical love once. Would it be greedy to expect to feel that way again?

Maybe nice is good enough.

A pounding on his kitchen door brought him out of his thoughts. He glanced at the clock—twelve thirty a.m. "Who on earth could that be?" he asked Sam. He had a feeling that if Sam could have shrugged, she would have.

The pounding started up again. Ryan walked over to the door

and flipped on the outdoor light. He smiled when he saw who it was through the window and opened the door. "Hi, Kristen. You're home early from your date."

Kristen's eyes flashed at him as she put her hands on her hips. She was still wearing her evening gown. She looked like an angry fairy, which only made Ryan smiled wider.

"What is wrong with you?" she demanded. "How could you say what you did to Bradley?"

Ryan's brows furrowed. "What? You mean about him being your father?"

Kristen took a step closer and pointed her finger at him. "You know damned well that's what I mean. Why would you say a thing like that? You knew he wasn't my father. It was mean and insulting, and just downright rude! You only said it to get back at me for calling Nichole your daughter."

Ryan held back a laugh as he tried to look contrite. It was hard, though. Her eyes were so damned beautiful when she was angry. He cleared his throat. "You're right. It was mean. I'm sorry."

"You're damned right I'm right," she said. Then she stood there, seemingly lost over his apologizing.

"But you did give me a hard time that first day we met and you called Nichole my daughter," he said.

She frowned. "Well, what was I supposed to think? She's so much younger than you."

"And Bradley is so much older than you are."

Kristen's face grew red. "That's none of your business. He's a well-respected neurosurgeon and a very nice man. You shouldn't have insulted him like that."

Ryan hadn't known he was a surgeon. That explained the BMW. "Again, you're right. I'm sorry, Kristen. I was only teasing you, but it wasn't very nice. Truce?"

Kristen crossed her arms. "No. No truce. I'm still mad at you."

Sam poked her head around Ryan's legs, her ears back.

"I think Sam's upset from all the yelling," Ryan said, patting her on the head.

Kristen's face softened. "Sorry, Sam. I'm not mad at you. Just at your owner."

Sam's ears perked up.

Kristen pointed her finger at Ryan. "But I'm not letting you off the hook," she said, then turned and started to walk away.

"Kristen?"

She stopped and turned around. "What?"

"You look beautiful tonight."

She stood there for only a second, a surprised look on her face. He saw her give a hint of a smile before she headed through the bushes to her place.

Ryan grinned as he closed the door. "She did look beautiful, didn't she, girl?" he asked Sam.

Sam only smiled back.

* * *

Kristen stomped into her kitchen and slammed the door. Sitting down in a chair at the table, she fumbled with her shoe straps until they were finally off and breathed a sigh of relief. She hated wearing heels!

She picked them up and walked upstairs, fuming about Ryan. All night long she'd thought of nothing else except what he'd said about Bradley being her father. It had ruined her night, even though it hadn't seemed to bother Bradley at all. She couldn't let it go. *How dare he think Bradley was my father!*

She undressed and slipped into cozy pajamas and fluffy slippers. As she slowly pulled the pins from her hair and shook it out, she thought about tonight and how courteous Bradley had been to her. He made sure to include her in all conversations and even when his doctor friends talked about work, he kept her apprised of what they were discussing. He was polite, kind, and sweet.

So why am I here alone tonight and not with him?

After he'd driven her home, Bradley walked her to her door. He declined her invitation to come inside and gave her a chaste kiss goodnight.

"I have rounds at the hospital early in the morning and then a golf date with some friends at noon," he'd told her in his gentle voice. "Otherwise, you know I'd love to stay."

Actually, no, she didn't know that he'd love to stay. They'd spent the night together only a few times, and even then, he left before morning arrived. No snuggling, no breakfast in bed. They'd been dating a few months by then, and when he finally slept over, she thought it might be the start of a strong relationship. But it hadn't been. She didn't doubt that he was dating her exclusively, but he had such a busy schedule and an active social life that there wasn't much room in it for nights with her.

But did she mind?

Bradley was a handsome man. He kept his body in good shape and had a lot of energy. He was gentle and considerate. But the few times they'd been intimate, well, she had to admit there hadn't exactly been fireworks.

But at this stage of the game did she need fireworks?

This train of thought was getting her nowhere.

As she crawled into bed, she thought once again about her exchange with Ryan earlier.

She's so much younger than you.

And Bradley's so much older than you are.

She understood the double standard there. She thought Ryan was a dirty old man for dating Nichole, but here she was, dating a man who was twenty years older than she was. Still, Ryan shouldn't have insulted Bradley. He was the innocent victim in all of this.

As she drifted off to sleep, her last thought was of Ryan, standing in the doorway, saying, "You look beautiful tonight." And for reasons she couldn't explain, that made her smile.

* * *

Ryan stood on Kristen's back porch and knocked softly on the door. Sam was standing on the step behind him, behaving so well that it made Ryan think she knew something was up. He hoped that Kristen was no longer angry with him for the night before. He thought that inviting her for a walk might help smooth things over.

The door opened and Kristen narrowed her eyes at him. Then she looked down at Sam, smiled, and said, "Hey, girl. How are you this morning?"

Sam strutted past Ryan and into the kitchen where Kristen kneeled down and pet her behind the ears.

"Okay. I get it. You're still angry with me," Ryan said.

Kristen looked up at him. "I should never talk to you again."

Ryan nodded. "I understand. But you could just as easily not talk to me while we're walking to the park, can't you?"

Kristen frowned and then turned her attention back to Sam. "Do you want to go for a walk, girl?"

At the word *walk,* Sam began to dance around Kristen.

"Okay, okay," Kristen said, laughing. "I'll get my sweatshirt."

Sam followed Kristen out of the kitchen and up the stairs, leaving Ryan still standing outside on the back porch.

"Sheesh. I guess I'm the dog today," he muttered.

They headed down the street and turned toward the park. Kristen held Sam's leash and walked two steps ahead of Ryan. The day was beautiful with a soft breeze and the new green leaves on the trees swayed gently above them. Ryan thought it was the perfect day for a long walk and would be better if Kristen would at least let him walk with her.

"I said I was sorry," he called out to her. "What more do you want me to do?"

Kristen turned and looked at him but continued walking. "We'll see," she said, then grinned.

Ryan took long strides and caught up with them and finally the three were together on the sidewalk. Children played outside on their lawns, some rode their bikes on the sidewalk, while others ran around playing tag. When they got to the park, they turned right and headed north on the path as they had done before.

"What type of soup are you making this week?" Ryan asked, trying to find a way to start up a conversation between them again.

"I'm not making soup this week. I'm making chili. I thought it sounded good."

"It does sound good. I like chili."

Kristen slid her gaze over to him. "Are you hinting you'd like a jar of chili?"

Ryan grinned. "I'm not hinting. I'm saying it outright."

Kristen laughed. "You sure take the cake, you know that?"

"I'll have a piece of that too, if you're making it."

"We'll see," she said.

"About the cake?"

She hit his arm. "No, silly. About the chili. We'll see if you can behave yourself through the walk."

They walked for a while and then turned around and headed back. Ryan felt relieved that Kristen was talking to him again. He enjoyed their friendship and didn't want to lose it over something stupid he'd said.

As they headed home, Kristen spoke up. "I get it, you know.

About the double standard."

Ryan stared at her. "What?"

"I get it. I gave you a hard time about dating younger girls, but I'm dating a guy who's a lot older than me. I shouldn't have judged you for it. I'm just as terrible as you." She looked at him, her eyes sparkling mischievously.

Your eyes are beautiful. The thought popped right into Ryan's head, and for a moment, he was afraid he'd said it out loud. He was relieved when Kristen didn't react.

"I guess we're both terrible people," he said, smiling. "So, you forgive me?"

Kristen laughed. "I guess so." Her smiled faded. "But I do have my reasons for dating an older man. I was already married to someone my own age and it didn't work out. I trust Bradley. He's…dependable."

Ryan glanced over at Kristen. He thought she deserved so much more than just *dependable.*

"I'm sorry your marriage didn't work out. I'm sure Bradley is a good guy, too."

Kristen nodded. "I haven't seen Nichole around lately. Are you still seeing her?"

"Actually, I'm not sure. I've tried calling and texting her, but she doesn't answer. She's the free spirit type. But I did meet another woman last night who you might actually approve of. She's closer to my age. I think I'll be seeing her again."

"Oh." Kristen glanced down at the sidewalk. "Well, that's nice."

Ryan thought her voice sounded funny and wondered why. But before he could ask, his phone buzzed in his pocket. He pulled it out and saw it was his dad. "I'm sorry. I have to take this. It's my father."

"Of course," Kristen said, walking a little ahead of Ryan to give him privacy.

"Hi, Dad. What's up?" Ryan said, figuring his father was just checking in as he did on most Sundays. But his smile faded when he heard what his father had to say. After a few minutes of conversation, Ryan told his father he'd get there as soon as he could and said goodbye.

He hurried to catch up with Kristen.

"Is everything okay?" she asked.

"No. I'm sorry, but I have to get home quickly. I have to try to catch a flight home today."

"Oh, Ryan. What happened?" she asked as they quickened their steps.

Ryan stopped and looked down into Kristen's eyes. "My mother had a mild heart attack. My dad says she's doing fine, considering, but the doctor's worried about her heart now. They're doing some tests."

"I'm so sorry, Ryan. Let's get you home so you can get ready to leave. Your family needs you there."

They walked quickly back to his house and when he got there, Ryan stopped and stared at Kristen. He felt completely overwhelmed and had no idea what he needed to do first.

Kristen must have seen the lost look in his eyes because she went to him and wrapped her arms around him. "Take it one step at a time," she said softly.

He reached around her and pulled her close. Her nearness made him feel stronger, as if he were drawing strength from her. Her hair was soft against his neck and she had a light, sweet scent about her. He held her for what seemed like a long time, yet it was probably only a few seconds. Sam came up beside him and sat, rubbing her nose along his leg as if to say she was there for him, too.

Ryan reluctantly pulled away. It had been a long time since he'd had someone to rely on, and in that one hug, he felt as if he could count on Kristen to do just about anything for him.

"Why don't you pack a bag and I'll check on flights for you?" she said. "Do you have a computer I can use?"

Ryan nodded and led the way into the house. He pointed out the laptop on the kitchen table and Kristen immediately went over to it and started looking up flights.

"Go on. Pack. I'll take care of this," she said.

He ran upstairs and found a small suitcase, then began tossing clothes into it. He had no idea how long he'd be gone or how much he should take, then he realized he could buy whatever he needed if necessary.

He changed into a fresh pair of jeans and a polo shirt and slipped a light sweater over that. When he got downstairs, Kristen already had three different flights figured out for him with or without a rental car.

"The three o'clock will be fine," he said. "And I'll need a car. I don't want to bother my dad or sister to come get me at the airport." He handed her his credit card.

Kristen finished booking the flight and printed out the ticket and information on the printer beside the table.

"Here it is," she said, handing it to him. He'd just finished talking to Jon to tell him he'd be away from work for a few days.

"Thanks, Kristen," he said, giving her a small smile. "You've been such a big help. I think I would have panicked without you here."

"You would have been fine. And don't worry about the animals. I can feed them for you, if you'd like. Just tell me how much and how often you feed them."

He hit the side of his head with the palm of his hand. "I forgot all about the animals. The Finleys always fed them for me."

"Well, I'm here now," she said softly. "That is, if you trust me to take care of them."

Ryan looked into her blue-green eyes, the eyes he'd thought

were so beautiful just an hour ago. He barely knew her, but he felt as if he'd known her for a long time. He trusted her completely. "Of course I trust you," he said. "How could I not, after all you've done for me?"

She smiled. "You need to go. Give me a key and tell me what to do so you can get out of here. Your mother needs you now."

Ryan showed her where the canned food was and told her how often he fed the cats and Sam, and then they walked out to his car in the driveway.

"Let me know how she's doing, okay?" Kristen asked as he put his suitcase into the back seat.

"I will. Wait, I need your number," he said. He handed her his phone and she put her number into it. "I'll be sure to call as soon as I know anything."

Kristen nodded, and then as if it were the most natural thing in the world, she hugged him again and wished him a safe flight.

As Ryan drove away, he thought about how lucky he was to have Kristen as his neighbor.

Chapter Ten

Ryan spent more time in the Minneapolis-St. Paul International Airport checking in than he did on his flight to Cedar Rapids. By four forty-five, he was already in his rental car driving toward the hospital. His father didn't have a cell phone, so he'd called his sister, Stacy, to let her know he was on his way.

When he arrived at the hospital, he went directly to room 303 where Stacy had told him to go. She was standing outside the room when he arrived, and she smiled wanly and hugged him close.

"I'm so glad you're here," she said, sounding relieved despite her steadfast nature. Stacy was as no-nonsense as his mother, and always seemed on top of everything, but between caring for her two children and worrying about their mother's health, Ryan was sure she was exhausted.

"I came as soon as I heard. How is she?"

"Mom's actually doing quite well considering how weak she is. The doctor said that sometimes chemo treatments can weaken the heart, and he's taking her off her treatment plan for a few weeks. He wants her to build up her strength before continuing."

Ryan shook his head and ran his hand through his hair. "So, either the cancer will kill her or the treatments will. Kind of a hard choice to make, isn't it?"

Stacy placed her hand on his arm and locked eyes with him.

"It is hard, but Mom is doing all she can to be with us as long as possible."

Ryan sighed. "I know. Can I go in and see her?"

"The doctor's in there right now. As soon as he's through, we can go in."

"Where's Dad?"

"I made him go home for a little while to sleep. He would be here the entire time if he could, but that's not good for him, either. Thank goodness school lets out soon so he can be with her for the summer. Otherwise, I think he'd go crazy with worry."

Ryan nodded. His parents had the type of marriage that everyone dreamed of. They'd been at each other's side for forty years and they were the most compatible couple Ryan had ever known. He had found that same type of perfect love with Amanda and thought he'd have it forever, like his parents. But nothing lasts forever, as his loss of Amanda, and now his mother's illness proved.

He glanced at his sister and saw how tired she looked, too. Her dark hair was mussed and there were circles under her blue eyes. "Maybe you should take your own advice and go home for a while. You look beat."

Stacy laughed. "Gee, thanks big brother. So, you're telling me I look old and haggard?"

Ryan smiled. "No, you are as beautiful as always. But it can't be easy for you to spend so much time here and then go home to those two little adorable girls of yours. How are they, by the way? I'll bet they're growing like weeds."

"Yes, they are. They're doing great. Gerald took them to a movie today to keep them occupied. Tomorrow, though, I'll have to either find a babysitter or stay home. I'm hoping Mom will be able to go home soon so I can bring the girls there and help Dad out."

"I wish I could help more," Ryan said. "I feel bad that it's all left for you to do."

"Don't feel bad. I'm glad I can help as much as possible. And Mom loves having the girls around. Dad will be off of work soon and then he'll be around more to care for Mom."

Ryan nodded. His father taught high school mathematics in the same school his mother had retired from a year earlier. He planned on working one more year before retiring, but Ryan wondered if his dad might retire earlier to spend more time with Marla. Ryan wished he would. He was afraid his dad might regret it if he didn't take off that year earlier.

The doctor came out of the room and Stacy introduced Ryan to him. He explained that Marla was doing well and should be strong enough to go home in a couple of days.

"We want to monitor her heart another twenty-four hours. If all is well, we'll let her go home," he said.

Stacy and Ryan thanked him and he walked away down the hall.

"I'm going to take your advice and go home for a while," Stacy said. "Give Mom my love. I'll be back later this evening to see her."

Ryan hugged her goodbye and then took a deep breath before entering his mother's hospital room.

"Hey, Mom," he said, and she turned her head and smiled wide.

"Ryan. I'm so happy you're here. Come and give me a hug."

Ryan walked over to the other side of her bed and gently wrapped his arms around her. She was so much thinner since the last time he'd visited that he was afraid he'd hurt her. When he pulled away, he noticed how tired she looked; her hazel eyes were dull and her face had more wrinkles than he'd remembered. She was pale, and her once thick brown hair with silver running through it was gone.

"Now don't give me that look, sweetie," she said, her voice weak but still authoritative. "I know I look old and worn out, but I still have a lot of fight in me."

Ryan smiled. "I know you do, Mom."

"Sit down and tell me what's new in your life," Marla said, pointing to the chair beside the bed.

Ryan sat and told his mother what he'd been doing these past few weeks. Halfway through, he realized she'd easily diverted the subject of her health to him. It was so like her to be more interested in what others were doing than talk about herself.

"I didn't come here to talk about me," he finally said. "Tell me how you're feeling."

Marla waved a slender hand through the air to brush his concern away. "I'm fine, didn't anyone tell you that? I only did this so you'd fly here to see me." She grinned, and Ryan smiled back.

"I'm happy to hear that you're seeing other women again. You know that I loved Amanda dearly, but you're too young to live your life alone. So, tell me more about this woman you met the other night."

Ryan told her what little he knew about Christy, and then filled her in on his new neighbor and how sweet she was to watch his animals for him while he was away. "Kristen's a pediatric oncology nurse. Can you imagine how tough that would be? She's so self-assured and strong-minded. And she adores Sam, which is wonderful for me. Did I tell you she takes Sam walking almost every day?"

"She sounds wonderful. It makes me wonder why you aren't dating her."

Ryan stopped and stared at his mother. "Why do you say that?"

"You're so animated when you talk about Kristen. Plus, she loves older homes, she sounds like a hard worker, and she loves pets. She's perfect for you."

Ryan laughed. "We're just neighbors, Mom. Besides, she's already dating someone."

Long after he left to let his mother rest and drove to his parents' home, Ryan couldn't get his mother's words out of his head. *She's perfect for you.* He liked Kristen and enjoyed her company, but he hadn't let himself consider anything beyond that. Besides, he knew there was no way he could compete with Dr. BMW. He was sure he made more money in one operation than Ryan did for the entire year.

When he got to his parents' house, his father was already up and ready to go back to the hospital. It was past seven, but James wanted to see Marla before she fell asleep for the night. Ryan marveled at his parent's devotion to each other. As he settled into his room, he could only hope that one day he'd find someone again to be as devoted to as his father was to his mother.

* * *

Monday afternoon, Kristen was surprised to get a call from Bradley asking if she'd like to have dinner that night. She said she'd love to, so he picked her up at six o'clock and took her to a nice little restaurant they'd dined at before. It was upscale but not too much so, and Kristen was happy she'd worn a dress and heels. Bradley usually dined at fine restaurants, so she'd anticipated she'd need to dress up.

After their drinks had arrived and they'd ordered their dinner, Bradley spoke up. "I felt bad about leaving you so early Saturday night. I wanted to make up for it by taking you to dinner."

Kristen had wondered why he'd called on a weeknight. They usually only went out on weekends because of his hectic schedule. "You didn't have to do that," she told him. "But I'm glad you did. We don't spend enough time together."

Bradley gave her one of his charming smiles in return and it reminded her just how handsome he was. Since Saturday night, she hadn't been able to get their age difference off her mind— all because of Ryan. Sure, her sister teased her all the time about Bradley's age, but it wasn't until Ryan said something that it had actually bothered her. But looking across the small table at Bradley now, she remembered why she'd been attracted to him in the first place. He was polite, kind, and very, very handsome. He also knew who he was and where he was headed in his life— actually, he'd already arrived at his destination in life and was comfortable with it. All of those attributes made him a hundred times better than any man her own age. They all seemed to be trying to find themselves.

Still, that twenty-year age difference gave her pause.

"Is something bothering you?" Bradley asked. He'd been telling her about the surgery he'd performed that day, but stopped and stared at her curiously.

"No. Nothing is bothering me," she lied. "My mind is somewhere else."

Their food came and they ate in between discussing their work. Kristen liked that she could talk about her job with Bradley. He understood how difficult it was to work with terminally ill patients, and especially with children. He'd said more than once how much he admired her for what she did. Not just anyone could take care of ill children, and she appreciated that he acknowledged it. Of course, not many people could do what he did, either.

After dinner, Bradley drove her home and she invited him in for coffee. He turned on her stereo while she made them each a cup and they settled onto the sofa as the soft music drifted through the air.

"Can I ask you a question?" Kristen asked, turning to him.

Bradley chuckled. "You sound so formal. Of course you can."

"Do you think that our age difference is a problem?"

Bradley stared at her a moment. "No, I don't have a problem with it. Where is this coming from?"

Kristen let out a breath that she hadn't even realized she'd been holding in. "Oh, I don't know. It's just that people always mention it to me, and now I'm second guessing our age difference."

"Does it bother you?"

"No, not really. It never did. Oh, forget I mentioned it. It was a silly question."

Bradley stared at her curiously. "Is this because your neighbor called me your father?"

Kristen winced. If she were honest, she had to admit that was the reason it was bothering her. But it sounded ridiculous to worry just because Ryan had teased her about it. "No, it isn't," she lied. "And I'm sorry about him saying that. He was giving me a hard time and it was rude."

"Well, I'm not worried about our age difference," he said, pulling her to him and kissing her softly on the lips. "We have a nice, comfortable relationship. I'm happy with it as long as you are."

That night they made love, slow and sweet, the way Kristen loved it, and Bradley even stayed and pulled her close to snuggle afterward. Kristen enjoyed how comfortable they felt with each other, but she questioned if it was enough. Wasn't that the word Bradley had used to describe their relationship? Comfortable? Is that all she wanted? No sparks, no fireworks, just nice and comfortable? After her divorce, all that had sounded good. A nice, successful man she didn't have to support and a steady relationship. But now, she wondered if there might be more out there, somewhere, for her. As she lay in Bradley's arms, listening to the steady rhythm of his breathing as he slept, her mind drifted to Ryan and she wondered what he was doing right now, and how his mother was.

* * *

Tuesday morning Kristen woke up to an empty spot beside her. Bradley must have gotten up very early and quietly left. She lay there a moment, almost relieved. Then she felt guilty. Kristen sighed. "What's wrong with me?" she asked aloud to the empty room.

She remembered she had to feed Sam and the cats, and her mood lifted. Kristen glanced at the clock. It was only seven a.m. She had to be to work at noon, so she had plenty of time to take Sam for a walk before she had to get ready to leave. That brought a smile to her face. Walking Sam was the highlight of her day.

She quickly dressed and headed over to Ryan's house to care for the animals. The cats were waiting expectantly for her at the kitchen door. They apparently didn't care who fed them their meal—they just wanted to eat. Sam was happier to see her. She sat behind the cats and smiled, her tail thumping on the tile floor.

Kristen scratched her behind the ears and then ran down the hallway to unlatch Sam's doggie door. Sam slipped out and returned to the kitchen just as Kristen placed her food bowl down on the floor.

Kristen's cell phone buzzed in her pocket, startling her. She pulled it out and saw the call was from Ryan. She smiled, then immediately frowned. *It's just Ryan, for Pete's sake.*

"Hi," she said when she answered.

"Good morning. I hope I didn't wake you."

"Of course not. I'm over at your place, feeding Sam and the cats. How's your mother?"

Ryan explained that she was feeling better and that she'd be going home later that afternoon. "They're delaying her chemo for now, until she's stronger."

"That's good," Kristen said, although she understood the implications of stopping the treatments. It meant the cancer could grow quicker, but she hoped that wasn't the case. "I'm sure she'll be better very soon."

Ryan was silent a minute. "She's the strongest woman I've ever known," he finally said. "I'm hoping for the best."

Kristen's heart went out to him. His voice was unsteady, as if he could break down at any minute. She suddenly wished she was there with him. "Me, too," she said softly.

Their conversation turned to the animals and the weather— safe subjects. Ryan told her he'd be flying in late Wednesday night because he couldn't miss any more work. They hung up soon afterward, with Kristen telling Ryan that she'd be sending positive thoughts his mother's way.

After the call, Kristen felt lost for a moment. She felt so helpless here when Ryan was going through so much back home. *But it's not your problem, remember? He's just your neighbor.*

Kristen sighed then she saw Sam sitting down beside her and she smiled. "Let's go for a walk, girl," she said, her spirits already lifting. She snapped on Sam's leash and they headed out the door.

Chapter Eleven

Ryan hung up the phone feeling better after having talked to Kristen. *I'll send positive thoughts your mother's way* she'd said before they'd ended the call. Her words warmed his heart. She'd never met his mother, and if truth be told, she hardly knew him, but her words were heartfelt.

It's because she's a nurse, you idiot. This is what she does for a living.

Still, it made him feel better.

He showered, dressed, and headed downstairs for a bite to eat. He found the kitchen empty with only a note on the counter from his father.

"Off to the hospital to see your mother and then to work. See you later, Dad."

Ryan smiled. His father was just as amazing as his mother. He made sure to see her each morning before work. Ryan and Amanda had been that way. They'd always eaten breakfast together before he headed to his office and she started her workday. Often, they'd meet downtown for lunch, if she could manage it between appointments, and always ate dinner together. Making time for each other had been paramount in their relationship. Ryan loved the time they'd spent together. He only wished they'd had more.

Ryan drove to the hospital thinking again about his conversation with Kristen. She was so easy to talk to that it surprised him. He didn't have to force a conversation or come up with topics. Their conversation flowed easily, and he liked that.

She's perfect for you. His mother's words echoed in his head. Right. Because Kristen would definitely drop a doctor— correction, a brain surgeon—to be with a guy like him. He chuckled as he stepped off the elevator and headed to his mother's room.

"What's that grin for?" Stacy asked when he walked into the room. "You look like the cat who ate the canary."

"I had toast for breakfast, not canary," Ryan teased as he kissed his sister on the cheek and then his mom. "How are you today, Mom?"

"I'm doing fine, dear. Almost as good as new," Marla said. Although Ryan noted that she still looked pale and tired. "I'll bet that grin is for one of your many girlfriends."

Ryan snorted as he sat on a chair by the bed. "Yeah, because I have women all over me. I'm just beating them off with a stick."

"Just don't scare away that sweet neighbor girl of yours," his mother said. "I already like her and I haven't even met her yet."

"Neighbor girl? What neighbor girl? Are you seeing someone and I don't know anything about it?" Stacy asked, clearly surprised.

Ryan shook his head. "No, I'm not seeing anyone. Well, no one seriously, and definitely not my neighbor." He frowned. "Well, I mean I *see* her, and we go for walks with Sam, and she's taking care of my pets while I'm gone, but we aren't *seeing* each other."

Marla laughed. "So, she's watching your pets, you go on walks together, but you're not interested in each other at all. Hmmm, sounds a bit fishy to me."

"Sounds like the start of a relationship to me," Stacy said, eyeing him. "Why didn't you tell me?"

"Because it's not a relationship," Ryan said, exasperated.

"Is she cute?" Stacy asked.

"Well, yeah, she's very pretty."

"Is she nice?" Marla added.

"Yes, of course she's nice." He couldn't help but grin. "I just spoke to her this morning—about the pets, so don't get that look on your faces—and she said she'd send positive thoughts your way, Mom. She has a kind heart."

Stacy and Marla looked at each other, then at Ryan.

"What?" Ryan asked, wondering about their conspiratorial look.

"So, what's wrong with her?" Marla asked.

Ryan frowned. "Nothing's wrong with her."

"Then why don't you want to date her?" Stacy asked.

Ryan just sat there, staring at his mom and sister. They sure knew how to turn a guy inside out when they wanted to. And for the life of him, he had no idea how to answer that question.

"It's not a matter of wanting to date her," he finally said. "She's already seeing someone—a surgeon. So dating her isn't an option, okay?"

Marla shook her head. "Such a shame. She's perfect for you."

Ryan laughed. "You two are too much," he said. "How did I ever survive growing up with you two giving me the third degree all the time?"

"That's what little sisters are for," Stacy said, grinning.

"And mothers," Marla said.

They visited a while longer until Marla grew tired. Stacy left to run errands before she had to pick up her girls from preschool and kindergarten. Ryan stood to leave, too, so his mother could nap. He told her he'd be back later, after she rested.

"Ryan?" Marla said, her voice quiet.

"Yeah, Mom?"

"You know that I only want the best for you, don't you, dear?

I worry about you being alone. Amanda and you were the perfect couple, and I adored her. I'm so afraid that you might not open yourself up to finding someone else."

Ryan took his mother's hand. "You don't have to worry about me, Mom. I'll find someone to share my life with someday. No one can ever take Amanda's place, but I'm sure there's someone out there, somewhere."

"Sometimes, dear, everything we're looking for is right in front of us."

"Let's just get you feeling better, Mom. Then you can worry about me, okay?"

As Ryan drove to his parent's house, he thought about his mother's words. *Everything we're looking for is right in front of us.* He knew she was talking about Kristen. There she was, right next door, single—sort of—cute, nice, and fun to be around. But he knew she wasn't even slightly interested in him. They were friends, or at least building a good friendship. He couldn't ask for anything more than that.

* * *

Wednesday afternoon, Kristen came home from work, changed into jeans and a sweatshirt, and headed over to Ryan's house to feed the cats and take Sam walking. It gave her a warm feeling inside when she saw how excited Sam was to see her after a long day of work. Sam rushed to the door and her tail wagged with pure delight.

"Gee, if only I could find a man who was that excited to see me," Kristen said, laughing. She fed the cats and was soon outside with Sam, walking through the neighborhood.

The day was gloomy and cool, but that didn't stop Kristen. Taking a walk after work helped her to decompress and burn off stress. Today had been a tough. A little boy she'd known for the past two years died, and try as she might to stay strong, it was heartbreaking. She tried not to get attached to her patients, but it was difficult. Working with them week after week, year after year, she couldn't help but become attached. She was relieved today when her shift was over and she could finally come home and spend time with Sam.

"Hello, Kristen. I see you're out for a walk again." Ruth waved from her porch, so Kristen walked up the sidewalk to say hello.

"Hi, Ruth. Yeah, I'm taking Sam for a walk, or she's taking me, I'm not sure." Kristen laughed.

"I haven't seen Ryan around. Is everything okay?"

"He went to visit his mother in Iowa. She's not doing too well."

"Oh my. I'm sorry to hear that. He's such a nice young man. And his wife was so sweet. I really miss her. I'm glad you moved in. We needed a smiling face around here. You bring joy to the neighborhood."

Kristen smiled. "Thanks. That's nice of you to say."

"Well, tell Ryan when you talk to him that I'm thinking about him. I'll keep his mother in my prayers."

"I will. I'll see you later." Kristen waved as she walked away.

Kristen's mind wandered as she walked. She felt so lucky to have found a nice house in a place where her neighbors were so friendly. Ruth was such a sweetheart, and Ryan? He was nice too, well, when he wasn't insulting Bradley. Thinking of Ryan, she wondered when he'd be flying in today. She hadn't talked to him since yesterday morning. Maybe she could call him, just to ask, and then she thought better of it. If he wanted to let her know when he was flying in, he'd have texted or called her.

So why are you disappointed that he didn't?

"That's okay," she said aloud to Sam. "You and I can spend the evening together until he gets home. How does that sound?"

Sam smiled and wagged her tail. Kristen took that as a yes.

* * *

Ryan headed back to the hospital after three o'clock to visit his mother a while longer before he had to fly home. He thought she'd have been sent home already, but then figured she'd waited for his dad to get off work and pick her up. But when Ryan walked toward his mother's room, he saw his father standing in the hallway with a worried look on his face.

Ryan quickened his steps. "Hey, Dad. Is something wrong?"

James looked up at him. "Your mother is having complications. Her heart started having abnormal rhythms, and the doctor was concerned the damage was greater than they first realized. They've taken her for some tests, and it looks like she won't be coming home for a few more days."

Ryan stared at his dad. His mother was talking and joking just this morning. How could she not be well now? "I'm so sorry, Dad. Come, let's sit down and wait."

They sat in the hallway while doctors and nurses buzzed around them, as visitors came and went, and patients were brought up to rooms. None of it fazed the two men in the plastic chairs. Both were thinking about Marla.

"Did the doctor say what happened? Was her heartbeat slow? Fast?" Ryan wanted to know.

James sighed. "Her heart monitor displayed irregular heartbeats. Plus, her pulse was very slow. The nurse noticed it when she checked on her this afternoon. I don't know much more than that. The doctor said he'd fill me in when the tests were complete."

Ryan nodded. He looked at the time. He was supposed to take the six o'clock flight out to Minneapolis, but he didn't want to leave until he knew his mother would be okay. Checking his phone, he saw there was a nine o'clock flight, so he changed it.

Stacy came in a while later and a worried frown crossed her face when she saw the two men sitting in the hallway. "What's wrong?" she asked her dad.

He filled her in and she grabbed a chair and sat with them. "I don't understand it. She was doing so well this morning. And she looked so good," Stacy said.

Ryan agreed. "I thought for sure she'd be going home by now."

Finally, Marla was brought back to her room in a wheelchair and the nurse helped her into the bed. James was at her side immediately, tucking the blanket around her as Stacy and Ryan stood close by.

"What are all the long faces for?" Marla said. "I'm fine." Although her weak voice and paleness told them otherwise.

The doctor came in and explained the situation. "I want to keep Marla here a few more days for observation. If her heart rhythms are consistent, then she can go home."

Marla sighed. "A few more days. I so wanted to go home."

The doctor smiled. "I know. I promise I won't keep you any longer than necessary."

After the doctor left, Marla turned to Ryan. "I thought you were flying home today. Don't you have a big meeting tomorrow?"

"I couldn't leave without knowing how you were," Ryan told her.

Marla waved her hand through the air. "Oh, pish. It was just a blip. Don't worry about me. I'm not going anywhere for a very long time."

Ryan smiled and shook his head. "Well, you sound fine, that's for sure."

Everyone laughed.

After visiting a while longer, Ryan finally tore himself away from his family and kissed his mother goodbye. "I wish I could stay a few more days. I'll call you tomorrow to see how you're doing."

"Don't worry about me, sweetie. You need to get back to your own life. Say hi to that sweet neighbor of yours, okay?" Marla winked.

Ryan laughed and promised he would. He hugged his father and sister goodbye and headed out the door. Stacy followed him to the elevator.

"Let me know if anything changes, okay?" Ryan said to her. "No matter what time of day or night, I want to know."

Stacy nodded. "I will. This new problem scares me. The cancer was hard enough to deal with, but a weakened heart on top of it is even scarier."

"I feel the same way. Mom's strong, though. She can fight this."

He hugged his sister again and stepped into the elevator. As the doors closed, he waved one last time. He had tried to put on a strong front for Stacy, but inside he wasn't as sure as he'd sounded. He prayed that this wouldn't be the last time he saw his mother.

Chapter Twelve

Kristen awoke suddenly to the sound of a car door shutting in the driveway. She shook the cobwebs from her head and looked down on the floor by the sofa. Sam was lying there, staring back at her.

"I'll bet that's Ryan," she told the dog. She glanced at the clock in the living room. It was after eleven. Kristen couldn't believe it was already that late. She and Sam had come back to her house after their walk, made dinner, gone over to feed the cats again, and then returned to the house to relax and watch a little television. Kristen had enjoyed Sam's company, even if the conversation was one-sided. At least she was someone to talk to—and she was a good listener.

Kristen stood and stretched, then clicked off the television. "We'd better get you back to your owner," she said, looking at Sam. She bent down and pet her head. "I'd love to keep you overnight, but Ryan probably wouldn't appreciate my stealing his dog."

Sam only smiled.

Kristen grabbed a sweatshirt and slipped on a pair of sneakers. On impulse, she took a jar of chili out of the refrigerator to bring over to Ryan. Then she and Sam headed next door.

Ryan opened the kitchen door on the first knock. He was

still wearing his coat and his bag was on the floor. Sam ran in and jumped on Ryan, happy to see him. Ryan pet her a moment, then told her to get down. "Hey, girl. Glad to see you, too."

"Hi. I thought you might like your dog back," Kristen said, smiling. But when she saw the tired look in Ryan's eyes, she immediately became concerned. "How's your mother?"

Ryan sighed and ran his hand through his hair. "She had a setback today, so they're keeping her in the hospital a few more days."

"Oh, Ryan, I'm so sorry," Kristen said.

"I felt terrible about having to leave, but I didn't have a choice. I have a presentation planned for tomorrow and it's with the type of customer you don't want to ignore. But it was hard saying goodbye."

"Can I do anything to help?"

Ryan shook his head. "I'm going to get these guys fed and go to bed. Thanks so much for taking care of them, Kristen. I don't know what I would have done if I hadn't had your help."

"I enjoyed it," she said. "Here, let me take care of the animals and you can put your stuff away. Are you hungry? I could make you something."

"That's nice of you, but I'm fine. If you don't mind feeding the pack, though, I'd appreciate it." Ryan walked out of the kitchen with Sam at his heels and Kristen heard him drop onto the sofa in the living room. She quickly fed the cats and washed out their bowls when they were finished. She set the jar of chili in the fridge to stay fresh. When she finally peeked out into the living room, she saw Ryan lying on the sofa, facing away from her. Sam had taken up residence on the floor beside him.

"I'll be leaving now," Kristen called out, but there was no reply. She stepped into the room a bit farther, and that's when she heard the steady sound of breathing. Ryan had fallen asleep on the sofa.

Kristen took a few more steps closer to Ryan and gazed down at him. His hair was mussed, and there were dark circles under his eyes. Her heart went out to him. It was hard seeing anyone suffer, especially a close relative. She was sure he was worn out from worry for his mother.

Kristen tip-toed up beside the sofa, putting her finger to her lips when Sam looked up at her. Sam must have understood to stay quiet, because she put her head down again and closed her eyes. Reaching over Ryan, Kristen pulled the blanket off the back of the sofa and unfolded it. She gently laid it over him, careful not to wake him. As she gazed down at him, she thought how handsome he was, despite looking tired. And he cared so much about his family, which she found heartwarming. Ryan really was a nice guy. Without even knowing why, she bent down and placed a soft kiss on his cheek.

"Goodnight Ryan," she whispered. Then she patted Sam on the head and quietly let herself out of the house.

* * *

Ryan awoke early the next morning on the sofa with Punkin sitting on his chest, staring at him. He glanced around, confused. Had he really slept on the sofa all night?

"Okay, boy, okay," he said, lifting Punkin up and setting him on the end of the sofa. Sam sprung up from the floor, grinning happily because Ryan was awake.

Ryan patted her on the head. "I must have been beat to sleep here all night," he told Sam. He ran his hand through his hair, and then realized there was a blanket covering him. He didn't remember pulling it down.

"I think I'm losing my mind," he said. "Well, I'm talking to animals, so I'm sure my mind is already lost."

He got up and stretched and headed for the kitchen to feed

everyone. When he opened the fridge to get out Sam's canned food, his eyes landed on the jar of chili, and it all came rushing back to him.

Kristen.

He'd been wiped out by the time he'd come home last night from the long day and the flight, but mostly from worrying about his mother. By the time he'd driven home from the airport and walked inside the house, he was dazed. He did remember Kristen bringing Sam over and even offering to make him something to eat. After that, it was all a blank.

He set the food bowls down for the animals and gazed out into the living room at the blanket still on the sofa. Had Kristen covered him up? He must have fallen asleep before she left.

Funny, because he'd thought he'd dreamt that someone had bent over him and kissed his cheek. It had felt nice, comforting. But it was a dream, right? Kristen wouldn't have kissed him.

"You are losing your mind," he said.

Remembering he had an important meeting today, he hurried upstairs to shower. It was going to be a very long day.

Over the next two days, Ryan kept in constant touch with his sister, texting back and forth about his mother's health. The doctors let her go home on Friday, which was a relief, but Ryan knew she still had a long road to travel. Once her heart situation was stable, she could start chemo again. It was all so unbelievable to Ryan that good people like his mother had to endure so much pain.

By Friday night he was exhausted so he skipped his workout and headed home. Besides, he knew Jon would bother him about hitting the bars and he really didn't want to. He needed to decompress from his stressful week.

As he pulled into his driveway, he realized he hadn't seen

Kristen over the past two days. He knew she'd walked Sam every day, but their paths hadn't crossed. So, after he changed clothes, he and Sam walked over to Kristen's and knocked on her kitchen door.

She answered it in her usual jeans and sweatshirt. Her hair was pulled back in a ponytail and her face was free of make-up. Ryan smiled. He thought she looked adorable.

"Hi. I hope we're not bothering you," Ryan said, as Sam walked into the kitchen, making herself at home.

"No, not at all. Come on in," Kristen said.

Ryan stepped into the kitchen. "I just dropped by to thank you again for taking care of the animals."

"I was happy to do it. How's your mother doing?"

"They sent her home today, so that's a good sign," he said, leaning against the kitchen island.

Kristen smiled. "That's great. I'm happy to hear that."

Ryan gazed around Kristen's kitchen, once again reminded of Amanda.

Kristen cocked her head. "What are you thinking?"

"Oh, sorry. I dazed out a moment. I was just remembering when Amanda redecorated this kitchen. It had been all black and white, with checkerboard floors and tile counters—very 1950s. The Finleys loved the new kitchen she designed for them."

"I love it, too. Your wife was very talented. And beautiful."

Ryan's brows raised.

"Oh, sorry. I couldn't help but see the photos of her on the hutch when I was over last night. You two were a lovely couple."

"Thanks. And sorry about falling asleep last night while you were still there. I was bushed," Ryan said.

"No problem."

Ryan stood there a moment, then asked, "I know this is a weird question, but do you think it's strange for me to still have pictures of Amanda around the house?"

"No, not at all," Kristen said, looking surprised. "You and she were together a long time. It's only natural you'd have photos of her around the house. Why? Did someone say something?"

"Yes, but it's more than that. I guess that now that I'm dating again, it could put some women off to see pictures of my wife."

"Well, that's their problem, not yours. If you get married again, you may want to pack them away, but until then it's no one's business. I think it's heartwarming how much you loved her. A lot of married couples don't have what you two did."

Silence fell around them and Ryan figured it was time to leave. "I should let you get back to what you were doing. Come on, Sam. Let's go home."

Sam's head perked up from where she was lying on the floor by Kristen, but she didn't get up.

"Oh, there's no hurry for you to leave, unless you have somewhere to go. I wasn't doing much of anything. I was just wondering what to have for dinner. I'm kind of tired of soup and chili."

Ryan shrugged. "I don't have anywhere I have to be. Hey, I have an idea. Do you like subs?"

Kristen nodded. "Sure."

"Why don't we grab a couple of subs and drive to the park and sit there while we eat? That way Sam can come along, too. There's this great local place that makes the best subs."

"Sounds good to me," Kristen said.

They headed out to his car and Sam jumped into the back seat. Ryan drove a few blocks and stopped at a small shop that made subs and pizza. When their order was ready, they hopped back into the car and headed over to the park. While Ryan drove, Sam was sniffing the air, a big smile on her face.

"Not for you, girl," he said, laughing.

Sam looked disappointed.

At the park, they found a table near the lakeshore and settled in. Sam lay down on the grass beside them as they ate.

"So, it's Friday night. Why aren't you out with Dr. Methuselah?" Ryan said with a wicked grin.

Kristen scowled at him. "I could ask you the same question. Why aren't you out with the teenybopper?"

Ryan laughed and raised his hand up. "Okay, okay. I won't say anything more about Dr. BMW if you'll leave Nichole be."

Kristen laughed too. They talked about safe topics, like the park, the weather, and Sam.

"I've been meaning to ask you. What's that little cottage in your backyard for? It's adorable. Is it a guest house?" Kristen asked.

Ryan's smile faded. "It was my wife's office. Basically, it still is. I haven't cleaned it out yet. I keep thinking I should, but it's hard. It's the last place where I can go and feel her all around me. I can still smell her perfume and touch items she last touched." Ryan looked up at Kristen. "I know it sounds weird, but I can't help it. Someday, I'll be able to clean it out and say goodbye for good."

Kristen reached across the table and gently laid her hand on Ryan's arm. "Everyone grieves in their own way and their own time. Don't let anyone push you into getting rid of anything you're not ready to dispose of. When you're ready, you'll do it."

Ryan looked down into Kristen's eyes and felt the warmth of her words just as he felt the warmth of her hand on his arm. He nodded, unable to speak because of the lump in his throat. She was the first person to tell him this. Everyone else had pushed him to get rid of Amanda's things as soon as possible to wipe away her memory, as if that would wipe away the pain. But the pain of losing her couldn't be pushed away so easily. It felt good to hear Kristen tell him that he should go at his own pace.

The sun was slowly setting, leaving long, golden shadows on the lake. They threw away their garbage and started walking back to the car. As they did, it began to rain.

Ryan looked up, confused. "Where's this rain coming from?"

"That one little dark cloud above us," Kristen said, pointing to it. At that moment, the gentle rain turned into a downpour and the trio ran to the car. They were all soaked by the time they were inside.

"This is crazy," Ryan said, laughing. He was dripping wet with nothing in the car to dry off with. He glanced at Kristen, who was equally wet, but she was laughing too.

"Good thing you have that seat cover for Sam. She's drenched."

Just as Kristen said that, Sam began to shake and amidst their protests, water sprayed all over them. Then Sam sat on the seat and smiled.

When they got home, the sun was almost down and there was a chill in the air. Despite being wet, Ryan walked Kristen to her kitchen door and waited while she unlocked it.

"Thanks for the sub," Kristen said. "This was fun."

"Even with getting wet?"

Kristen nodded. "Yeah, even with that. We'll have to do this again sometime."

Ryan stood there a moment, staring down into her eyes. She was soaked, her ponytail was dripping, and yet she looked adorable. He had an overwhelming urge to kiss her. And for a moment, he thought he saw in her eyes that she wanted to also.

Sam barked playfully. The moment evaporated.

"Guess I'd better get her dried off," Ryan said.

"Yeah. She's pretty wet." Kristen walked inside, then turned back. "Wait a minute. I almost forgot." She ran off for a moment and returned with a small envelope addressed to "Kristen's Cute Neighbor."

"What's this?" Ryan asked, confused.

"My patient, Gabbie, the little girl I told you about who loves dogs, wanted to invite you and Sam to her birthday party tomorrow. Sorry for the short notice, but she just gave it to me yesterday."

"Why me?" he asked. "I've never met her."

"Mostly because she'd love to meet Sam, but she didn't want you to feel left out."

Ryan smiled. "That's sweet of her. Sam will love it." Then he looked at the envelope again. "Kristen's Cute Neighbor?"

Kristen bit her lip and her cheeks turned pink. "I told her your name but she was being a little imp. She asked me about my new neighbors and then if you were cute or not."

"I see. Well, I guess I know what your answer was."

Kristen's cheeks turned a darker shade of pink.

"I can't wait to meet her. I'll see you tomorrow." Ryan turned and walked through the bushes to his house with Sam at his heels. He opened the door and walked in, nearly tripping over the two cats waiting for him. When he looked down, he saw he was dripping on the rug. He was wet and cold but he barely noticed because of the warmth he felt inside.

Chapter Thirteen

Kristen thought about the evening as she showered and dried off. It had been fun spending time with Ryan and Sam tonight. It was always so easy being around him. She hadn't even minded getting wet when that strange little storm appeared. And when he walked her over to her door, for an instant, she'd thought he was going to kiss her. If truth be told, she almost wished he had.

"It's best that he didn't," she said aloud with a sigh. After all, he had Nichole and she had Bradley, and a kiss would complicate everything. She smiled to herself. It sure would have been nice, though.

As Kristen readied for bed, she was excited about tomorrow. She adored Gabbie and couldn't wait for Gabbie to meet Ryan. And she knew that Gabbie couldn't wait to see Sam. Watching her eyes light up with excitement would be fun. Gabbie didn't have much in her life to make her smile, so tomorrow would be extra special for her.

Once in bed, Kristen thought back to last night and the kiss she'd given Ryan. She pondered why she'd felt the urge to do it. At the moment, it had seemed like the most natural thing to do, but thinking back, she had no idea what possessed her. True, she was a caregiver by nature and profession, and she'd so wanted to ease his pain in that moment. But she cared for children all day, every day, yet she'd never kissed any of them on the cheek.

It could be you have feelings for him.

Yikes! Where did that come from? Although, she *had* wanted him to kiss her tonight.

Kristen rolled her eyes at herself. "Go to bed and stop thinking crazy thoughts."

Yet even as she drifted off to sleep, all Kristen could think about was Ryan's delicious chocolate-brown eyes.

* * *

The next morning, Kristen stayed busy doing laundry and chopping vegetables for the chicken and rice soup she planned on making on Sunday. By one o'clock, she was dressed and ready to go to Gabbie's party when there was a knock on the door. When she answered it, there stood Bradley.

"Bradley?" Kristen said.

"It looks like I surprised you," he said with a smile. He walked inside, giving her a quick kiss as he passed her.

Kristen turned and watched as he walked inside and took off his jacket. "You sure did. Why are you here?"

"I came to take you to your patient's party. Remember when you told me about it last week?"

Kristen nodded. "Yes, but you said you were golfing with friends today, like you do every Saturday."

Bradley grinned. "Well, I decided I'd rather spend the day with you. It sounded like this patient was very important to you and I wanted to share today with you."

Kristen stood there, dumbfounded. She was touched that Bradley had taken the time away from his beloved golf to put her first. However, she was also a little disappointed. She'd been looking forward to spending the day with Ryan and Sam. Before she could say anything, another voice startled her.

"Are you ready to go? I thought we could ride together."

Kristen turned to see Ryan on the porch with a smile on his face. Sam took the open door as an invitation to go right in, so she did, heading straight for Bradley.

"Oh," was all Kristen could manage to get out before Sam leaped up on Bradley, leaving wet paw prints on his tan trousers. "Down, girl!" Ryan yelled once he saw the situation. He ran inside and grabbed ahold of Sam's collar, pulling her off of him. Bradley backed away quickly, nearly tripping over the sofa.

"I'm so sorry," Ryan said to Bradley, as the latter began brushing off his pants. "Sam believes that everyone is a dog person."

"Yes, well, that's fine," Bradley said, looking more than a little perturbed. "I'll just go and wipe it off in the bathroom." He left the room briskly, possibly in fear of another dog attack.

Ryan turned and looked over at Kristen. "I didn't realize he was coming, too."

Kristen heard the disappointment in Ryan's voice and she felt terrible. "I'm sorry. I didn't realize he was coming either," she said quietly so Bradley wouldn't hear. "You'll still come, won't you?"

Ryan nodded. "Of course. I wouldn't want to disappoint Gabbie."

Kristen's heart swelled with gratitude. Any other guy wouldn't have gone, but he was doing it for Gabbie. "Thank you," she said.

"No problem. So, I guess I'll see you there."

"Yes. We'll be right behind you."

"Come on, Sam," Ryan said, tugging at her collar, and they disappeared out the front door.

Kristen sighed. She felt like a little piece of her went out the door with them.

"Ready to go?" Bradley asked, coming up behind her. He glanced around. "Did your neighbor leave already?"

"Yes," Kristen said. She picked up her gift for Gabbie off the hall table and then followed Bradley out to his BMW.

* * *

Ryan was disappointed to say the least. He'd been looking forward to spending the day with Kristen. But that went down the tubes when Dr. BMW appeared. "You shouldn't have jumped up on the old guy's pants," he admonished Sam. Then a wicked grin appeared on his face. "But I'm sure glad you did," he whispered to Sam.

Sam only smiled.

He and Sam hopped into his car and headed across town to where Gabbie's party was. They arrived twenty minutes later. It was a beautiful day so the park was crowded with parents and children. Ryan found a parking space at the far end of the lot. No sooner had he left the car and snapped on Sam's leash than a black BMW pulled up beside his car. Kristen got out quickly and headed over to Ryan. Bradley stayed in the car. It looked like he was talking on the phone.

Kristen nodded toward Bradley. "He's on the phone with the hospital. The story of his life. I told him I was heading over to the party."

Ryan grinned. At least he had Kristen to himself for the time being. He handed her Sam's leash and the three of them made their way through the throngs of people.

Children laughed with glee on the swings while others ran around large oak trees in a game of tag.

"Sam is in her version of heaven," Ryan said. "So many children, so little time."

Kristen laughed. "She does love children. I've noticed that on our walks. I have her full attention until a child walks by."

"Yeah. She would have made a great family dog," Ryan said,

a sharp pang of grief lacing his words. He hadn't meant to sound that way. Kristen stared at him curiously, but didn't say a word.

Up ahead was a large group of people with four picnic tables pulled together. Blue, pink, and yellow balloons hung everywhere and the tables were covered in colorful cloths.

"There they are," Kristen said, her face breaking into a wide smile. Her steps quickened and so did Sam's. Ryan hurried to catch up.

They walked through the group of parents and children. Some of the people greeted Kristen like an old friend. Everyone bent down to pet Sam, and she lapped up all the attention like she was the guest of honor. As they neared the center table, that's when Ryan saw the birthday girl sitting serenely in a pretty green dress. Her brown eyes followed Sam and there was a sweet smile on her lips. Her hair was gone, but she didn't need it to look beautiful. She was lovely just as she was.

Kristen walked up to Gabbie and gave her a hug while Ryan lingered behind, holding both his gift and Kristen's. Sam sat without being told and gently laid her head on Gabbie's lap. Ryan watched her, amazed. It was as if Sam sensed that Gabbie was the person she was here to see.

"Oh, Sam!" Gabbie exclaimed, wrapping her arms around her. "You're as beautiful as your pictures."

Sam sat there patiently and let Gabbie stroke her fur. Sam was a good dog, but Ryan had never seen her sit so quietly for so long. He was very proud of her.

"Gabbie, I'd like you to meet my friend Ryan," Kristen said.

Ryan stepped forward as Gabbie lifted her gaze. She had the most beautiful brown eyes he'd ever seen. They were a deep, rich color that shimmered in the light and he felt as if they were searching his very soul.

"Hi, Ryan. I'm Gabbie. It's short for Gabriella. You know, like the angel, Gabriel."

Ryan stood there a moment as he looked at Gabbie. There was an actual glow about her, as if she truly were an angel. He reached out his hand. "Happy Birthday, Gabbie. It's so nice to meet you."

Gabbie enclosed his big hand in both of her small ones. "I'm so happy to meet you, too." She stared at him intently. "Kristen was right. You are a nice man."

Her words took him by surprise. "Thank you," he said. Her hands slipped away and returned to stroking Sam's fur.

"No. Thank you for bringing Sam. Seeing her is the best present I've ever had."

"I was happy to do it for you," Ryan said, and then her eyes turned to Sam and whatever magic that was between them evaporated. Ryan blinked, not exactly sure what had occurred.

Kristen drew near him and said quietly, "She pulled you in, didn't she?"

Ryan stared at her. "Yeah. She did. What just happened?"

Kristen chuckled. "I can't explain it. There's something magical about her. She draws you in and you're hers for life. She's a very special person."

Ryan had to agree. But he thought that Kristen was also a very special person for noticing how amazing Gabbie was.

Ryan was introduced to Gabbie's mother and a few other relatives of hers and soon the cake was served and everyone sang *Happy Birthday*. Sam sat quietly beside Gabbie the entire time. Not long after that, Bradley appeared.

"I'm sorry I took so long," he told Kristen after nodding to Ryan. "I'm afraid something has come up and I need to go to the hospital. Are you ready to go home?"

Kristen looked disappointed. "But you haven't even met Gabbie yet."

"I'm sorry, Kristen. But I really must go."

Ryan hated for their day to end so abruptly. "I'll drive her home," he offered.

Bradley looked up at him, then back at Kristen. "Would you like to do that instead?"

Kristen nodded.

"Okay. Well, have a good time. I'll call you as soon as I can." He placed a kiss on her cheek, nodded again to Ryan, and was off.

Kristen turned to Ryan. "Thanks. He's always running off on emergencies."

"Well, he does have an important job. I guess that's to be expected." Ryan didn't know why he was defending Dr. BMW, but he felt as if he should say something nice about him. At least Ryan got what he wanted—to spend the day with Kristen.

They spent another hour at the party and then said their goodbyes. Kristen took a picture of Gabbie and Sam together before they left. Gabbie thanked Ryan again for bringing Sam and once again he felt a strong connection when their eyes met. Ryan understood that there was something special about Gabbie and he'd never forget her sweet face.

They drove home in silence, and even Sam was quiet in the back seat. When Ryan pulled up into his driveway, Kristen turned to him.

"It's been such a wonderful day. Would you like to come over for dinner? I hate to see this day end so soon."

"Sure, I'd love to. I'll just feed the cats and be right over."

Ryan hurried home and fed Sam and the cats. He ran into the bathroom and quickly smoothed down his hair and checked his teeth for food. Still not satisfied, he brushed his teeth and then changed his shirt. Looking into the mirror again, he laughed.

"Geez, you're acting like a teenager on a first date," he said to himself. Sam walked into the bedroom and stared at him. "It's just dinner with Kristen—my friend, right, Sam? So what am I getting myself so worked up about?"

Maybe because you have feelings for her, you idiot.

Ryan stared at Sam a moment as if the dog had said the thought that popped into his head.

Sam just smiled.

"She's involved with Dr. BMW," Ryan told Sam. "Kristen is off limits."

Ryan's excitement to have dinner with her faded. *We're just friends. We're just friends.* He repeated that mantra over and over in his mind as he and Sam headed back over to Kristen's house. But when he walked inside and saw her smiling up at him as she poured a jar of her homemade soup into a large pan on the stove, looking so cute and sweet, he immediately forgot that they were just friends. *Sorry, Dr. BMW. Every man for himself.*

They ate chicken noodle soup and homemade cornbread that Kristen had whipped up quickly and sat at the kitchen table overlooking the neighborhood. The two talked easily about Gabbie, Ryan's mother, and their jobs. Sam lay on the floor beside the table between their chairs. It was as comfortable as if they did this every night, and it reminded Ryan of all the homemade meals he and Amanda had shared in their own kitchen, just like this.

As if sensing Ryan's sudden turn of nostalgia, Kristen said, "Can I ask you a personal question?"

Ryan looked at her curiously. "Sure."

"Today when you said Sam would have made a great family dog, I could sense it upset you. I'm assuming you and Amanda wanted children but hadn't had them yet. Were you waiting to have children?"

Ryan slowly shook his head. "We wanted children very much, but unfortunately it never happened. We tried for years and even went through tests to find out why she wasn't getting pregnant. There was nothing wrong with either of us, so the doctors had no answers. They suggested fertility treatments but Amanda said no. She said she didn't want the stress of it all. If we were meant to have a baby, then it would happen. Otherwise, we'd consider adoption."

"How did you feel about that?" Kristen asked.

"I was fine with whatever she wanted, and I liked the idea of adoption. But we never had the chance to try."

"Do you mind if I ask how Amanda died? She was so young. Had she been sick?"

Ryan sat there a moment, staring down at his empty bowl as all the memories of the day Amanda died came flooding back to him.

"I'm sorry," Kristen rushed to say. "I shouldn't have brought it up."

Ryan looked up at her and shook his head. "No, it's fine. I was just remembering. She hadn't been sick at all. Amanda was healthy and young and full of life. It was a Sunday and we'd just come home from walking to the park with Sam. Amanda had run upstairs to change clothes so we could go out to eat, and I was downstairs, feeding the animals. Then Amanda called down to me to bring up a sweater that was hanging in the laundry room. I headed upstairs with it a minute or two later, and there she was, lying on the floor, motionless." Ryan stopped a moment to take a breath. The memory of Amanda lying on their bedroom floor was still etched in his mind. He looked up into Kristen's green-blue eyes and drew strength from the compassion he saw in them. "I went to her immediately, but it was already too late. She was gone. One moment she was alive and the next, gone. It was so difficult to comprehend. Even Sam was confused. She curled up beside Amanda on the floor, waiting for her to get up, and Sam wouldn't move until the paramedics took Amanda away. It was all so heart-wrenching."

"I'm so sorry, Ryan. Do you know what caused it?"

"A brain aneurism," he said. "It killed her instantly. Her father died the same way when he was only fifty-two, but no one ever thought that it could happen to Amanda. She was healthy and took such good care of herself. It was just so unexpected."

"Oh, Ryan. That's so sad."

Ryan nodded. "It's actually a relief talking about it. People think I should just get over it and move on. They don't understand that because her death was so unexpected, it's still hard for me to process it. But you work around death all the time so you understand how difficult it can be."

"Yes, I do. And even if you know someone is dying, it still comes as a shock. Death is sad no matter how it happens."

Ryan gazed at Kristen. "You're thinking of Gabbie, aren't you?"

"Yes. She's so incredible. She's been through so much in her short life, yet I've never seen her angry or discouraged. She has an inner-strength well beyond her years. And a deep faith that keeps her moving forward." Kristen smiled. "Sometimes I truly believe she has an angel on her shoulder. A special angel that whispers sweetness into her ear. Maybe it's even Gabriel, the messenger angel who she says she's named after."

"I think you're right," Ryan said, once again feeling the warmth he'd felt when he met Gabbie. "There is definitely something ethereal about her. She nearly glowed when I first saw her. There's something very special about her."

Kristen gazed up into his eyes. "I could tell that you felt it, too. Bradley thinks I'm silly when I speak about Gabbie that way. He doesn't see anything past scientific fact. But you do."

"Sometimes you have to believe in more than you can see or touch. Otherwise, life would be a sad, boring existence."

Kristen smiled. "So you still believe in Santa and the Easter Bunny?"

Ryan laughed. "You bet. I don't want to miss out on free

presents and candy."

They both laughed, lifting the mood. Ryan helped Kristen stack the dishwasher, and then she suggested they go sit on the porch since it was such a nice night.

Kristen had two rockers so she and Ryan sat side-by-side with Sam on the floor at their feet. The sun had already set and the streetlights gave a warm glow to the night sky. The sound of children playing in their yards had subsided as they went inside for the night and only the occasional bark of a dog in its yard broke the silence.

It was simple pleasures like this that Ryan missed, along with watching a movie with someone and snuggling on a Sunday morning. He turned and looked at Kristen, wondering how Dr. BMW could pass up spending a day with a woman as amazing as her. The guy might be a brain surgeon, but he was an idiot when it came to matters of the heart.

"Can I ask you a question now?" Ryan said.

Kristen turned to him and grinned. "Uh, oh. Okay. I guess it's only fair."

"Why Bradley? He's too old for you, he's too full of himself, and he doesn't give you the attention you deserve."

Kristen stared at him a moment, her expression serious. For an instant, he thought she was going to get up and go inside. Instead, her face softened and she said, "Because he's stable, he already knows who he is, and he's a lot more attentive to me than you realize."

"Sorry," Ryan said. "I just don't see you two as a couple. You're warm-hearted and compassionate. He's not. You deserve someone who appreciates you for who you are."

Kristen's eyes dropped to her lap. "If you knew what my life's been like up until now, you'd understand why stability is so important to me. My marriage was nothing like yours. My husband was lazy and obnoxious and had no problem sitting around playing video games or hanging out at the bar and letting me support him. He 'couldn't find his calling in life.' Can you imagine that? I told him he could work somewhere while he was waiting for his 'calling,' but he didn't appreciate that very much. As the tension grew between us, he added to it by sleeping with anyone who'd say yes. Add that to the fact that my own father left us when I was eight, never to be seen again. I don't put a lot of faith in men."

"I'm sorry, Kristen. You deserved so much better from both of them."

Kristen sighed. "Well, you can now understand why stability is important to me. And maturity. If nothing else, Bradley is secure and dependable."

The sorrow in her voice broke Ryan's heart. He reached over and placed his hand on her arm. "But is that enough?" he asked quietly.

Kristen looked up at him. "It has to be, for now."

Ryan stared into her eyes, his heart aching with sadness for her. It wasn't fair that an amazing woman like her had to settle for the wrong man just because others hadn't appreciated how special she was. He could see it in her, so why hadn't they? The depth of her eyes drew him nearer. His hand slid up her arm and behind her neck. Her hair felt silky to the touch. Without a second thought, he pulled her to him and their lips met.

Chapter Fourteen

Kristen hadn't even realized that Ryan was going to kiss her until their lips met. And once they touched, she couldn't resist. His lips felt warm against hers, and when his tongue found hers, delightful chills ran down her spine. She loved the feel of his hand on her neck and she reached up and cupped his face, wanting to touch him, too. When the kiss ended, she pulled away slowly and took in a quick breath of surprise. No one had ever kissed her with such passion as Ryan had, and she was struck by how much it stunned her.

Ryan's hand slowly fell away from the back of her neck, and she was sorry it was no longer there. He gazed at her, as if to register her reaction.

"I hadn't planned on doing that," he said softly. "But I'm not sorry I did."

Kristen wasn't sorry he had either.

Before either could say another word, a car pulled into Ryan's driveway and honked. They both looked up suddenly, as did Sam.

"Who in the world...?" Ryan started to say but was cut off by a man yelling his name.

"Hey, Ryan, old buddy. Where are you?"

Ryan and Kristen both stood and walked to the side of her porch. There in his driveway stood a man and two women.

"Well, there he is, ladies. Ryan. Since you haven't come out to party with us, we thought we'd bring the party to you."

"Who is that?" Kristen asked Ryan softly.

"That's Jon, a guy I work with, and his latest girlfriend," Ryan told her, sounding annoyed.

"So, who's the other woman?"

Ryan turned to Kristen. "She's the girlfriend's sister. I think I mentioned her to you. Kristen, I had no idea they were coming over."

From the surprised look on his face when they drove up, Kristen believed that was true. What bothered her was who the other woman was.

By now, Jon had walked up closer to Kristen's porch. He was carrying two bottles of alcohol. "Come on, Ryan. Let's get this party started. Christy's been wondering why you haven't called her so I brought her to you."

Kristen watched as the younger-looking of the two women sidled up to Jon and wrapped her arms around him. The other woman stood over by the car, looking uncomfortable. Kristen figured that must be Christy. She suddenly remembered he'd mentioned meeting a woman closer to his own age. Kristen's heart dropped.

Kristen turned to Ryan. "I forgot you were dating her, too," she said. "You should go join your friends." She turned around and headed for her door.

Ryan followed her. "Kristen, it's not what you think," he said, but Kristen didn't give him a chance to finish.

"Go be with your friends," she said, and then went inside and softly closed the door.

Kristen stood with her back against the door, feeling anger rising inside her. *What an idiot I am, believing in Ryan.* He was the same man who only weeks ago she'd thought was a dirty old man for dating Nichole. How could she not have realized he'd been dating several women at once?

Walking to the kitchen, she started the teakettle for a soothing cup of tea. She hadn't even realized she was shaking until she pulled down a mug and it rattled against the counter. She grabbed it with the other hand to stop it from shaking. She couldn't tell if she was angry, hurt, or heartbroken. But it didn't matter—she hated feeling any of those emotions.

Tonight was the first time in years she'd let her guard down and shared her past pain with a man. And what happened? He'd disappointed her like every other man in her life. She'd never even shared her story with Bradley. He knew she was divorced, and that was it. He'd never asked her about it, and that had been fine with Kristen. But then she'd opened up to Ryan, trusted him, and look how that turned out.

Kristen took her mug of steaming tea upstairs and curled up on her bed in a puddle of blankets. She wished she had Sam lying beside her to comfort her. She thought about the wonderful day she and Ryan had despite the surprise visit from Bradley. Ryan had been so sweet to bring Sam to Gabbie's party and had been kind to Gabbie, too. He'd realized how special the young girl was, and that had made Kristen happy. She hadn't wanted their day to end.

And then there was the kiss. Kristen closed her eyes and remembered the feel of Ryan's lips on hers. It had been a warm kiss, a magical kiss, awakening long-dead feelings inside of her. Feelings that even Bradley had never unlocked. And it left her wanting for so much more.

"He's no different than any other man," Kristen said to the silent room. Hot tears formed in her eyes. The kiss had meant nothing to him. She was just one of many in his long line of women. Kristen wiped her tears and snuggled deeper into her bed. They were neighbors, nothing more. She should have kept it that way. From now on, she would. She still wanted to walk

Sam, and she'd even watch the animals when Ryan visited his mother in Iowa, but that was it. *And that's why I date Bradley. He never makes me cry.*

* * *

Ryan reluctantly went back to the house with the group and let them inside. The cats had been waiting by the door for Ryan's return but ran off, scared by the group of newcomers. Sam snuck off too and curled up in a corner of the living room so she could watch all the action.

Jon made a beeline for the kitchen cupboards and soon had glasses pulled down to mix drinks from the vodka and rum he'd brought. Alicia was immediately at his side, but Christy held back and stood in the doorway to the living room. Ryan scowled at Jon, angry beyond words about his interrupting his nice evening with Kristen.

"So, what'll it be?" Jon asked, glancing at Ryan. "Vodka Seven or Rum and Coke?"

"Neither," Ryan said curtly.

"What? It's not a party unless the host is drinking," Jon said, laughing.

Ryan could tell Jon was already lit up, and by the look of Alicia's red cheeks, she was probably as drunk as Jon. "I'm not the one having the party," Ryan said.

Jon ignored him. "What about you, Christy? What'll you have?"

"I think I'll pass, too," she said from her spot by the door.

Ryan turned and looked at Christy. Her arms were crossed and she looked upset.

"What a couple of party-poopers you both are," Jon said, then he and Alicia laughed as if he'd said the funniest thing in the world.

Ryan walked over and forced a smile for Alicia. "Why don't you ladies get comfortable in the living room and I'll round up some snacks," he said, gently taking her elbow and leading her to Christy, making sure they were both walking to the sofa. Then he dropped the smile and headed back to Jon.

"What in the hell were you thinking, coming here out of the blue? Did it ever occur to you that I had something else going on?" Ryan said angrily.

Ryan's tone didn't even faze Jon. "Hey, I just wanted to bring you some fun. Alicia's been on me about you not calling her sister, so I figured I could bring her to you. If I'd known you had something going on with your hot neighbor, I wouldn't have come here." Jon smirked. "So, how long have you been hitting that cute number?"

Ryan's anger boiled over. He grabbed Jon by the collar and pushed him up against the counter. "Don't ever talk about my neighbor like that again, you hear? Or any other woman. Understand?" he growled.

Jon's face turned white. "Okay, okay." Ryan let him go and backed away a step. Jon smoothed out his shirt as he tried to regain his composure. "I guess it was a mistake coming here. We'll get out of your way."

Ryan instantly felt bad about his sudden outburst of anger. He generally wasn't a man who resorted to physical violence, but Jon had pushed him over the edge. Even though Jon could be a jerk, he was his co-worker and sort of a friend. "Wait, no," Ryan said, calmer now. "Stay a while. You shouldn't be driving in your condition. Why don't we relax and have some coffee before you go?"

Jon looked at him warily. "Well, I'll stay a while, but no coffee for me. I'm fine." He lifted his glass to show Ryan what he was drinking, then headed out into the living room.

Ryan sighed. He started a pot of coffee and rummaged

around the kitchen for some food. He put some cheese and crackers on a plate and also grabbed a bag of chips, then brought them out into the living room. Jon and Alicia were sitting close together on the sofa and Christy was over by the hutch, looking at pictures of Amanda.

"Anyone for coffee?" Ryan offered as he set the food on the coffee table.

"I'd like some," Christy said. The other two ignored them as Christy followed Ryan into the kitchen.

"For the record, it wasn't my idea to come here tonight," Christy said as soon as they were alone.

Ryan poured them each a mug of coffee and handed it to her. "I know. This is the sort of thing only Jon would come up with. I'm surprised, though, that you got into the car with him when he's so drunk."

Christy sipped her coffee. "I didn't know he or Alicia were that drunk until after we'd started heading out here. In fact, I was all settled in for the night at my apartment, but Alicia kept calling me, telling me they were coming here and you wanted me to come, too. I believed them. But when I got into the car, I realized that they'd had one too many. Believe me, I was relieved when we pulled into your driveway."

"So, they lied to you to bring you here? That's even worse than I originally thought."

Christy frowned at him. She set her mug down on the counter. "Listen, I'll call a cab and get out of your hair, okay?" She pulled her phone out of her pocket but stopped when Ryan placed a hand on her arm.

"I'm sorry. Please don't. I didn't mean to come across like a jerk. Why don't we join them in the living room for a bit and then I'll drive you home?"

"Don't worry. That's not necessary. I can call a cab."

"Christy, please. I'll be happy to drive you home. In fact, I should drive Alicia home, too, and let Jon spend the night. He shouldn't be driving."

Christy conceded. She picked up her mug again and headed out to the living room with Ryan at her heels.

After finishing his one drink, Jon stood. "We should go," he said to Alicia. "We've bothered Ryan enough. Besides, it's not even midnight yet. We're missing all the fun at the bars."

Ryan stood also. "Jon, you shouldn't be driving. You've been drinking. Why don't you stay the night here and I'll take the women home?"

Jon brushed his hand through the air and started walking toward the kitchen. "That's silly. I'm fine. I can drive." Alicia followed him.

Christy walked behind Alicia and touched her arm to get her attention. "Alicia, don't go with Jon. Please. Listen to Ryan. Let him drive us home. Jon is in no condition to drive."

Alicia just smiled. "Don't worry so much, big sis. We'll be fine. Besides, I'll miss all the fun if I go home now."

Christy looked at Ryan and shrugged.

"Alicia, please. Let me drive you," Ryan said.

Jon was already in his car and Alicia only waved and walked out the door to join him.

"I'm not sure what we can do," Ryan said. "Should I stop them?"

Christy shook her head. "Once Alicia sets her mind to something, I can't change it. All I can do is hope she'll be safe."

Ryan watched as Jon backed out onto the street. He felt helpless. Damn that Jon! He should know better than this.

"They'll be fine," Christy said. "I have to believe that. Alicia's a grown woman. I can't control what she does."

Ryan sighed and turned toward her. "Yeah, I guess so. Do you want to sit a while and talk?"

"Actually, if you don't mind, could you drive me home?

Tonight has been a bust."

"Sure."

Ryan drove her home. They rode in silence until he pulled up to her building. "Sorry about tonight. I wasn't expecting company. I'm not much of a party person."

"I'm not either. I only came along because they told me you'd invited us to your place. I should have known better. I mean, if you'd have wanted to see me, you would have called me yourself."

"Sorry about that, too. I had a crazy week. I flew to Iowa to see my family because my mother is ill and then I had to catch up at work. By the weekend, I was shot," Ryan said.

"I'm sorry to hear about your mother."

"Thanks," Ryan said. "Maybe when things settle down, we can get together."

Christy stared at him a minute, her expression unreadable.

"What's wrong?" Ryan asked.

"I was looking at all the lovely photos of your wife when we were at your house. She was beautiful. I bet she was smart and talented, too. I have a feeling she's a tough act to follow."

Ryan frowned. "What are you saying?"

Christy lightly placed her hand on his arm. "I'm just stating the truth. I think you may not be ready to move on yet. And that's okay—you have a right to take as much time as you need. I'm not sure I'd be able to compete with your wife's memory. Or that I'd want to."

Ryan was stunned by her words. Yes, she was right, he was still holding onto the memory of his wife, but he was also willing to try moving on. "I'm making an effort to move forward. It's hard, though. You're right—she would be a tough act to follow. But I'd never want another woman to try to compete with her. When the right woman comes along, it won't be a competition."

Christy leaned over and gave him a kiss on the cheek. "I hope you find the right woman. I'm afraid that it's not me. I have my own issues to deal with. But you are a handsome, sweet guy, and it won't be hard for you to find Ms. Right." She stepped out of her car, gave him a small wave, and walked to her door.

Ryan watched Christy until she was safely inside before driving away.

He thought about what she'd said about having to compete with his wife's memory. Obviously, his wife's photos at the house had made her pause. He didn't consciously compare every woman he met to his wife, but it seemed that most women felt he did. Yes, Amanda had been incredible and he'd loved her very much. But he couldn't replace her. He wasn't even going to try. He understood if he found someone else to share his life with, theirs would be a completely different relationship. But it seemed that the fact he still had photos of Amanda said otherwise to everyone else.

Everyone except Kristen.

Kristen had told him he should take as much time as he needed. She wasn't intimidated by Amanda's photos. In fact, she'd been very complimentary of them.

She's not intimidated because she's not interested in you.

Ryan sighed. That was more than likely true.

When he arrived home, he wandered around the house, looking at all the photos of Amanda. There were several on the hutch, a couple hanging in the hallway, and one on the nightstand in the bedroom. One was their wedding photo and another was of them on a beach in Florida. His favorite photo was of her standing on a dock at Lake Harriet, her blond hair brushed back by the breeze and her blue eyes twinkling. He'd taken it the year before she died. Looking around, he began to understand what Christy meant. It might be overwhelming for a woman to have to see these every time she came over. It would feel like a competition.

Sam came over, wagging her tail. Ryan bent down and patted her head, rubbing her behind the ears. "We are still hung up on Amanda, aren't we, girl? Maybe it's time to put some of these away." It pained Ryan to say it out loud.

Looking at the clock, he realized it was after one a.m. It had been a long day, and he'd had such a good time with Kristen. But after the whole Jon debacle, he was drained. He headed upstairs, undressed, and slipped in between the sheets. Sam followed suit, lying down on her pillow, and Punkin and Spice hopped up onto the bed. After turning off the lights, Ryan's thoughts returned to Kristen and the kiss they'd shared tonight.

He'd enjoyed kissing Kristen. To his delight, Kristen seemed to enjoy the kiss as much as he did. She hadn't pulled away, but instead moved nearer. It had been an incredible kiss. Except for Amanda, Ryan had never experienced a kiss as delightful as theirs had been.

I'm falling for Kristen.

The thought startled him, but then a slow smile spread across his face. "I'm falling for Kristen," he said to Sam.

Sam lifted her head and stared at him.

Ryan laughed. "I'm falling for Kristen, Sam. Can you believe it?"

Sam gave him her usual smile, then laid her head back down.

Christy had been right. It would take a very special woman to follow in Amanda's footsteps. Kristen was that woman. He'd only known her a short time, yet she'd managed to find a way into his heart. But did Kristen feel the same way?

Suddenly, Ryan wanted to run next door and see her. Did he dare? He had to tell her how he felt. She must have wondered about the kiss. Forget Dr. BMW. As Ryan had said earlier today, "Every man for himself."

Ryan glanced at the clock and sighed. Kristen would think he was crazy if he came banging on her door at this time of night.

He'd wait until morning.

For the first time in years, Ryan fell asleep with a smile on his lips.

Chapter Fifteen

Ryan awoke early the next morning feeling happier than he had in a long time. He showered and dressed, fed the animals, and then waited impatiently for ten o'clock to arrive. He didn't think he should go over to Kristen's earlier than that on a Sunday morning.

As he waited, he thought about what he wanted to say to her. He couldn't just blurt out that he had feelings for her, could he? Or, maybe he should just take her in his arms and kiss her again—like a romantic movie. Or, maybe not.

"Help me, Sam. What should I say?"

As usual, Sam didn't have an answer.

"I'll just tell her I loved kissing her and that I care about her," he told Sam. "And hopefully, she'll feel the same way."

Sam smiled.

As soon as the clock hit ten, Ryan was out the door with Sam on his heels. He knocked on Kristen's door and she answered it almost immediately. She stood there with the door partially open but didn't offer for them to come in.

"Hi, Ryan. Sam. What's up?"

Ryan was taken aback. Kristen wasn't her usually cheerful self, and she didn't invite them in. "Hi, Kristen. I was wondering if we could talk a minute."

Kristen looked behind her at the stove, and then back at

Ryan. "I'm sorry. Now isn't a good time. I'm making soup and I have to keep an eye on the broth so it doesn't boil over."

Ryan's heart sank. "Maybe we could go walking in a little while? It's a beautiful day."

"I can't today. Sorry. Bradley invited me out to dinner and I have to finish the soup first. Maybe some other time, though?"

Ryan stared at her. She wasn't making eye contact and she hadn't even paid any attention to Sam. It was obvious something was wrong. "Are you angry with me about last night? We had such a wonderful day and evening together. I really enjoyed spending time with you."

Kristen shook her head. "No, Ryan. I'm not angry. I'm just very busy today."

"Are you upset that I kissed you?"

Kristen's shoulders sagged, but then the sound of liquid boiling over grabbed her attention and she ran over to the stove to turn it down. Ryan stayed on the porch. He didn't want to leave until he told her what he'd come to say.

Kristen came back to the door. "I'm not angry about the kiss," she said softly. "It just happened. It's not like it meant anything. Let's not complicate things. You're dating other people, and I'm dating Bradley, so it would be best if we didn't let that happen again. Let's go back to just being friends. I'm happy to babysit the animals any time you need me to and I'd like to keep walking Sam, if that's okay."

Ryan couldn't believe what he was hearing. "You want to be just friends?"

Kristen nodded. "Yeah. That's what we are, aren't we?"

Ryan stood there, unsure. He wanted to say "No! I feel so much more than that for you," but he couldn't get the words out. He swallowed the lump that had formed in the back of his throat and replied, "Sure. Yeah. Friends."

Kristen smiled. "Good. I'd hate to lose you and Sam as

friends. I really have to go now. I'll see you around, okay?"

"Yeah. See you around," Ryan said, turning and stepping off the porch as Kristen closed the door. All the excitement he'd felt earlier today evaporated as he slowly walked through the bushes to his house.

* * *

Kristen closed the kitchen door softly and let out a huge sigh. Her heart ached over the shattered look on Ryan's face when she'd said they should just be friends. She cared about Ryan—how could she not? He was a genuinely kind guy, not to mention, handsome. And if she were honest, she had no idea what would have happened last night if they hadn't been interrupted. The way he kissed her was unlike any kiss she'd ever experienced. It may have been difficult to stop with just one.

But what could he expect her to do? Fall for him? He was dating Nichole and had Christy on the side. Plus, how many other women? Kristen didn't want to believe it was true that Ryan could be juggling women, but that's what she saw. And she didn't want to be one of many.

Sighing, Kristen walked to the stove and stirred the broth, adding vegetables and chicken. All she had left to add was the rice, then she could pour the soup into jars and refrigerate it. She had a whole day to fill after that until Bradley picked her up for dinner. She wished she could have said yes to Ryan's offer of a walk, but it wasn't a good idea. The less contact they had, the better.

But no matter how hard she tried, her thoughts kept returning to the kiss.

* * *

Ryan couldn't believe how things had turned so quickly between him and Kristen. He'd thought that after last night, she might feel the same way he did. Unfortunately, she didn't. And now, she was putting as much distance between them as she could. It made his heart break just thinking about it.

But what should he have expected? For her to fall madly in love with him after only one kiss? They'd only known each other for a month. After all the time they spent together, it felt longer than that, but the truth was, they didn't know each other that well.

Then why do I feel like my heart has been crushed?

Besides, Kristen had Bradley. Why on earth would she choose Ryan over Dr. BMW?

Ryan walked over to the hutch and picked up one of his wife's photos. "I think you'd like Kristen," he said to her. "She's kind and warm-hearted and smart. If you were still here, you and she would probably be friends." Ryan sighed.

He bent down and pet Sam. "Come on, girl. Let's go for a walk to the park. Maybe it will clear my head."

He and Sam headed out the door.

* * *

Later that night, Bradley picked up Kristen and they went to one of her favorite restaurants for dinner. It was a nice, quiet place where you could have the best wine and food but not worry about dressing up. Kristen knew that Bradley had picked the place to please her. And when he apologized for leaving her early on Saturday, she understood why they were there.

"It's fine," Kristen said. "I had a good time at the birthday party and Ryan drove me home." She thought about how kind Ryan had been to Gabbie and the unexpected rain that soaked them, and she smiled.

"Well, I do feel bad about it," Bradley continued. "I realize I do that to you often, and you are always so gracious about it. I know how much that party meant to you, and I promise I'll try to be more sensitive in the future."

Kristen was surprised. Bradley had never seemed to care before about having to leave because of work. "Thank you for that, Bradley. I appreciate it. I do understand how important your job is and emergencies do happen."

"You've been very patient with me," Bradley said. "Even when I haven't deserved it. Many women wouldn't be, but you understand me because you work in the medical field, too. That's why we get along so well. We understand each other."

Kristen stared at Bradley, confused as to where all this was leading.

Bradley reached across the table and took Kristen's hand in his. "We've been seeing each other for almost a year now, and I hope you know that I have a deep affection for you, Kristen. I know you could choose just about any young man to be with, and I feel honored that you choose to spend time with me." Bradley pulled a small, velvet box out of his jacket pocket and set it on the table between them.

Kristen looked at the box warily. "What is that?"

Bradley smiled and his usually sharp, blue eyes actually twinkled. "Open it and see."

Tentatively, Kristen picked up the box and slowly opened it. Inside was an incredible diamond ring—a large cushion-cut stone set in platinum with smaller diamonds set around it. Kristen gasped.

"Kristen. I know you're wary of marriage, but I promise you that I would take good care of you and never be unfaithful. I think we could have a wonderful life together. Will you marry me?"

Kristen was stunned. This was the last thing she'd ever

expected. She looked up into Bradley's eyes and saw how sincere he was. Marriage. Did she want to marry Bradley? He was safe. He was secure. But not once had either of them said, "I love you." Was safe and secure enough?

"I can see I've stunned you with my proposal," Bradley said, chuckling. "I didn't mean to. But over the past few weeks, I've realized that I'll never find another woman as warm, caring, and understanding as you are. I don't want to lose you because I waited too long. Here, try the ring on, just to see how it feels." He reached across the table and pulled the ring from its case, then slipped it on Kristen's finger. It was a bit loose, but it fit.

Kristen looked down at the ring. It was absolutely beautiful.

"I don't know what to say," she finally said. "I never expected this."

"I realize that, Kristen. And I don't expect you to give me an answer tonight. Just wear the ring and think about my proposal. Follow your heart. You'd never want for anything, and we'd be good for each other. Take your time to think it over."

Kristen nodded, still dazed.

Later that night, Kristen stood in her kitchen, staring at the big ring on her finger. It felt heavy, like a weight. The weight of making a commitment. She took a breath as panic started to set in. Was she ready to make a commitment? And to Bradley?

She was relieved that Bradley hadn't been able to stay the night because he had an early surgery in the morning. It gave her space to think seriously about his proposal.

Glancing up, Kristen saw the light on in Ryan's kitchen across the driveway. He was probably feeding the cats one last time before bed. For an instant, she wanted to run across the driveway and bang on his door. She wanted to tell him how sorry she was for the way she spoke to him today. She didn't want to lose his friendship, or whatever it was they'd formed. But she knew she couldn't. Kristen had to keep a friendly distance between them if she still wanted to get along with him and walk Sam. Her heart couldn't afford to be broken when he decided he wanted one of the many other women he dated instead of her.

Sighing, Kristen headed upstairs and readied for bed. She wished she had Sam with her now, a furry friend to hug tight and tell her problems to. She slipped the ring off and set it in a decorative dish on the nightstand. Then she turned out the light, hoping that tomorrow everything would be clearer.

* * *

On Monday morning, Jon came over to Ryan's desk and apologized for Saturday night. "I shouldn't have barged in like that," he said. "Alicia and I had had a few drinks and we thought it would be a great idea to bring Christy over there. I realize how stupid it was, now. I hope you won't hold it against me. We meant well."

"Don't worry about it," Ryan said. "But honestly, man. You can't drive after you've been drinking. Especially with Alicia in the car. That made me angrier than you just showing up."

Jon nodded. "I know. I was being an asshole. I swear, I won't do it again. Besides, Alicia and I are over. We won't be seeing each other anymore."

Ryan's brows raised. "What happened?"

"I'm not really sure, but alcohol was involved. We started arguing at a bar downtown after leaving your place and the next thing I knew, she was in a cab and driving away. For the life of me, I can't even remember what we were arguing about."

"You should call her. Maybe she doesn't remember either."

Jon shrugged. "I think I should just leave it alone. Alicia's a great girl, but I'm thinking she's a little young for me. Man, I can't keep up with these young girls. I think it's time I start dating women my own age."

Ryan laughed. "Welcome to adulthood."

When Ryan arrived home that evening, he saw the black BMW in front of Kristen's house. Sighing, he went inside, fed the animals, and changed into sweats. Lying on the sofa with the T.V. going, he patted Sam when she lay down on the floor beside him.

"Guess it's just you and me, girl."

Sam didn't have an answer for that.

Chapter Sixteen

Two weeks later on a Friday night, Ryan flew to Cedar Rapids to visit his family for the weekend. His mother was feeling better and getting stronger, so her doctor was going to start her chemo treatments the following week. Ryan thought it was a good time to visit her before the treatments wore her down again.

He hadn't seen much of Kristen over the past two weeks, but he did talk to her to ask if she'd feed his cats and take care of Sam. She was happy to do it, and said she'd probably let Sam spend the night to keep her company. Ryan had to laugh to himself. *I'll bet Dr. BMW will love that.* But he kept that thought to himself. He was just happy to have someone who enjoyed taking care of his pets.

Ryan rented a car at the airport and headed out to his parents' house. As he stepped inside, a delicious aroma drifted to him from the kitchen. He found his mother in there, baking his favorite cookies—oatmeal chocolate chip.

"Ryan! You're home." Marla walked over and gave him a warm hug before returning to her baking.

"Hey, Mom. This sure is a nice surprise." He picked up a cookie and took a bite. "A delicious surprise. But shouldn't you be resting?"

"Oh, pish posh. I'm feeling just fine, thank you very much." She smiled at him. "It's a mother's prerogative to spoil her children."

Ryan laughed as he took another cookie. "And to make them fat." He looked around. "Where's Dad?"

"He's in the family room, watching television. Why don't you put your things in your room and then come down and we'll all have a nice visit?"

Ryan stowed his bag in his room and headed back downstairs into the family room. His father was watching a crime drama but turned it down when he arrived.

"So glad you made it," James said, getting up to hug Ryan. "You know, your mom made your favorite cookies."

Ryan laughed. "Yeah, I already filched a couple."

Marla came into the room and sat on the sofa beside James. "So, have you asked out that wonderful neighbor of yours yet?"

"Wow, you're not even going to give me a chance to settle in, are you? No, Mom, I haven't asked her out. I told you, she has a boyfriend."

Marla waved her hand through the air. "Boyfriend. That's not the same as a fiancé or husband. She's still available. And she's perfect for you."

Ryan laughed. "You've never even met her. How can you know she's perfect for me?"

"Because a mother knows these things."

James looked at them both, confused. "Did I miss something? You're dating your neighbor?"

"No, Dad. I'm not dating anyone."

"Yet," Marla chimed in.

They talked about everything that had been going on in their lives since he'd last visited. Marla looked over at James conspiratorially, and Ryan noticed.

"What's going on?"

Marla patted James's leg. "Your father has decided to retire a year early. That way we can spend as much time as possible together."

Ryan stared at his parents. He was happy his father had decided to retire early, but he also realized it was because his mother may not be here in another year, so James didn't want to wait. "That's great, Dad. You two can do a lot together."

"It was time I retired," James said. "Life's too short to keep working if you don't have to. We both have a nice retirement, and we'll be able to live comfortably for many years." James looked over at his wife. "Many years," he repeated.

Marla smiled and nodded. "Hey, I'm not going anywhere for a long time. I plan on traveling and spending all that retirement money."

Ryan chuckled. Nothing kept his mother down. But his dad was right—life was too short.

The next afternoon his sister, Stacy, her husband, Gerald, and their two girls, Lacey and Lilly came over for dinner. At three and five, Lacey and Lilly were the perfect age for Ryan to tease and tickle and play tag with out in the Collier's big backyard. When he stopped and sat down for a minute to have a beer, Stacy sat down next to him.

"You're just a big kid at heart," she said. "When are you going to finally ask your neighbor out so you can have a houseful of kids?"

Ryan rolled his eyes. "You too? Or did Mom tell you to bug me? I'm not dating the neighbor. She's taken."

"Who's taking care of your pets this weekend?"

"Kristen, my neighbor."

"Yeah, she's doing it out of the kindness of her heart, not because she's interested in you."

"No, she's just that nice, and she adores Sam."

Stacy shook her head. "Okay. It's your life."

"Thank you."

"Did Mom and Dad tell you he's retiring?"

Ryan's expression turned serious. "Yes, they did. I think it was a good decision."

"Me, too. It will give them time together."

Ryan turned and looked at Stacy. "How is Mom doing? Really. She changes the subject when I ask her."

Stacy sighed. "She's not in denial. She just doesn't want to talk about it and bring everyone down. Mom is keeping a positive attitude, and that's half the battle. But honestly, I'm not even sure. She seems strong now, after the heart attack. We'll have to see how she responds to the chemo treatments. If we're lucky, we'll have her here for a long time."

Later that night, after everyone had left, Ryan found his mother sitting at the kitchen table drinking a glass of milk.

"Hey, you caught me. I was going to sneak a snack," he said, getting a cookie. "I thought you went to bed already."

Marla laughed. "Some things never change. I tried, but I couldn't sleep. Today was a fun day, wasn't it? I love having you all home."

Ryan sat across from his mother. "It was. The girls are growing so fast. Sometimes, I think it would be better if I lived here, near family. But I love my job, too. It's hard being so far away, though."

"I think you are exactly where you're supposed to be, dear," Marla said. "Enjoying your work is important. It's such a big part of your life. And someday, hopefully, you'll find someone else to share your life with. That's important, too."

"It's hard, though, Mom. When I met Amanda, we had so much in common. Our ideals were the same and we both wanted to build a life together. Not all women are like that. Believe me, I've been trying to meet new women, but it's not easy. I think I'm too old fashioned for women today."

"That's silly. You're still young. I'm sure there's one woman out there who shares your same ideas about love, family, and relationships. You'll find her. Heck, she may be right next door." Marla winked.

Ryan groaned. "Not that again, please."

Marla patted his hand. "I'm just teasing you. But promise me you won't let life pass you by. Give love another chance. Amanda would want you to be happy."

"I know, Mom."

"Life's too short, dear. Just look at your dad and me. We thought we had years of retirement ahead of us to enjoy life. Now, maybe we do, maybe we don't. But at least we're going to try to enjoy what we have left together. Don't wait until it's too late. I want you to be happy, too."

Ryan nodded, a lump forming in his throat. His mother was right, no one could predict the future. He'd been holding back, comparing all women to his beloved Amanda. Maybe, it was time to let go and move on.

* * *

Late Sunday afternoon Kristen was finishing getting dressed to go to a late lunch with her sister when there was a knock on her kitchen door. She glanced out her bedroom window and saw Ryan's car in the driveway. "Your dad's home," she told Sam, who had been lying on the bedroom floor. They both rushed down the stairs and answered the door.

"Hi," Ryan said. "I'm home. I thought I'd take Sam off your hands." Sam jumped up and insisted Ryan pet her. "Hey, girl. You miss me?"

"She sure did. Come on in. Tell me how your trip went. How's your mother doing?" Kristen asked.

Ryan stepped into the kitchen. "She's doing well. We had a nice time. My sister and her kids came over on Saturday and we got to spend time together. It was fun."

"That's great."

"You look nice," Ryan said. "Are you going out?"

Kristen glanced down at herself. "Oh, yeah. I'm meeting my sister for a late lunch or early dinner. Not sure which. Nothing special, though."

"Oh, then I should let you go. Thanks so much for watching Sam and feeding the cats. I don't know what I'd do without you."

"You're welcome. I love having Sam here. She's good company."

Ryan stared at her a moment, and the smile on his face faded.

"What's the matter? Is my dress on backward?" Kristen teased, looking down.

"You're engaged?"

Kristen lifted her hand up and gazed at the ring as if she was surprised she was wearing it. Usually, she wore it only when she was with Bradley, but she'd put it on today to show her sister. Now, under Ryan's stare, the ring felt clumsy and awkward.

"Bradley asked me to marry him," she said, leaving out the fact that she hadn't accepted yet. After three weeks, she still hadn't decided.

Ryan's expression recovered quickly and she could tell he was forcing a smile for her. "Well, congratulations. He's a lucky guy."

"Thank you," Kristen said softly.

"I suppose this means you won't be living here much longer."

Kristen looked up, surprised. She hadn't thought that far ahead. "We haven't really discussed that yet," she said.

Ryan nodded. "I should let you get going. Thanks again for taking care of the animals. See you around." He whistled for Sam to follow and headed across the driveway and through the bushes.

"Yeah. See you around," Kristen said softly. Watching Ryan leave with Sam suddenly made her feel sad and alone.

* * *

Ryan walked into his kitchen, stopped, and leaned against the island, trying to grasp the fact that Kristen was engaged to Dr. BMW. It tore at his heart just thinking about it. He should have told her how he felt when he had the chance. Even when she was pushing him away, he should have blurted out how much he cared about her. But now it was too late. She was engaged.

Punkin and Spice came to greet him and Ryan fed them and Sam their dinner. He ran upstairs with his suitcase and unpacked it, then sat on the bed, staring at his wife's photo on the nightstand. By now, Sam had come upstairs and sat down on the floor next to him.

Ryan pet Sam's head. "Sorry, Sam. I should have told Kristen how I felt. Now, we've lost her. She'll probably move to some fancy downtown high-rise apartment. I'm sure Dr. BMW can afford only the best. I guess we should be happy for her." Ryan couldn't imagine ever being happy about Kristen marrying Bradley. Sam kept her opinions to herself.

Ryan's week went by quickly and before he knew it, the weekend arrived. He didn't mind being busy all week, because it kept his mind off of his personal life. But with the weekend looming ahead, he couldn't ignore that he'd be spending another weekend alone. It made him feel empty inside.

"You can come out with me tonight," Jon offered while they were in the gym Friday night. "We'll find a quiet place where the women are a little more mature."

Ryan shook his head. "No thanks. I'm not in the mood for

that tonight. Good luck."

Jon laughed. "I'll need it. You know, the reason I stayed away from older women is because they can see through my bullshit immediately. Guess I'll have to come up with a new game plan."

"Maybe you should just be yourself," Ryan suggested.

Jon pretended to shiver. "Now, that's scary."

Ryan walked into his quiet house and set his briefcase down. The cats and Sam were all waiting for him, so he served them dinner, then called his mother to see how her week went. She was in a good mood, despite starting chemo again.

"I'm feeling a little sick, but otherwise, I'm fine."

Ryan was glad to hear that and soon they hung up.

"Well, boys and girls," Ryan said to the animals. "I guess it's just us tonight. Who wants pizza?"

Sam would have said yes in a heartbeat, if she could.

Saturday morning, Ryan took Sam out for a long walk, staring longingly at Kristen's house when he passed it. Ruth was on her porch as Ryan walked by, and he waved at her.

"Isn't Kristen joining you today?" she called out?

Ryan stopped and shook his head. "No. Not today." He waved and kept on going. The last thing he wanted to do was try to explain to his neighbor why he and Kristen didn't walk together anymore.

"Do we even know why?" he asked Sam. "We went from friends to strangers in a heartbeat."

After their walk, they returned home and Ryan stood in the quiet house and wondered how he was going to fill the rest of the day. And night. Feeling lonely, he walked out into the backyard and to the cottage with Sam at his heels. He opened the door and stepped inside, taking in a deep breath. Then he frowned.

He no longer felt Amanda around him. Her scent, her presence. It was gone.

Ryan walked around the office space, looking at the last To-Do list she wrote for a project she'd been working on. *Gray tile, white marble counter, white cabinets.* Her handwriting was neat and precise, like she'd been. He looked around at the samples of wallpaper, carpeting, tiles, and flooring. Everything was stacked neatly and in order. But despite standing among the many items that Amanda had touched, in the office she sat in every day, Ryan no longer felt she was here.

"She's gone," he told Sam.

Sam looked up at him as if understanding.

Ryan sat heavily into the desk chair and Sam came over and placed her head in his lap. He stroked her fur as he tried to come to grips with this new realization. "Maybe she never really was here, huh, girl? Maybe I just wanted her to be so badly, I believed it."

They sat there a long time in silence as Ryan stroked Sam's fur. Ryan began to assess the room around him. It was a good size, and there was an attached bathroom that had hardly been used. There were big windows that brought in natural light. It would make a nice guest cottage. Perfect for his sister to use or his parents if they'd come to visit. He liked that idea.

Ryan stood and smiled down at Sam. "Girl, we have a lot of work to do. Let's go get some boxes and pack this stuff up. Then we can buy some new furniture for this room."

Sam looked up at him with big, sad eyes.

"It's okay. Amanda would like it if we made this into a nice place. That's what she loved doing, and I'm sure she'd approve."

With renewed energy at taking on a new task, Ryan closed the little cottage and he and Sam headed for his car.

Chapter Seventeen

Ryan spent the rest of the weekend packing up Amanda's office. He called a designer friend of Amanda to see if she or anyone else could use the sample books even though they were a few years old. She said she'd find a use for them. He decided he'd keep the desk and computer in there, and remove the rest of the items to make room for a queen-size bed and a sitting area. Next weekend he'd go furniture shopping to see what he could find.

Sunday evening as Ryan packed up the last of the boxes, he heard footsteps in the doorway. He turned at the same time Sam looked up. There stood Kristen.

"Hi. I hope you don't think I'm being nosy, but I noticed you've been out here all weekend and I wondered what you were up to."

Ryan smiled. She was wearing her usual sweatshirt and jeans, and her hair was up in a ponytail. She looked cute. "Come on in. Sam and I have been packing up the office. Well," Ryan laughed, "I've been packing and Sam's been watching."

Kristen walked inside slowly, looking all around. "Wow, you have been busy. This is kind of a big step for you, isn't it?"

Ryan nodded. "It's time. I've been holding on to this room so I wouldn't forget Amanda. But the truth is, I'll never forget her no matter how much of her stuff I pack away. So, it's time to let these things go."

Kristen walked over to Ryan and placed her hand on his arm. "That's good. It's healthy. And you're doing it your way, in your own time."

Ryan stood there, staring down into Kristen's eyes, feeling the warmth of her hand. It was all he could do not to bend down and kiss her. But she wasn't his to kiss. He stepped away. "Yeah. I'm going to make it into a guest cottage. I'm going furniture shopping next weekend. Get a bed, maybe a sofa and big comfy chair."

"Oh, that sounds like fun. I love shopping for furniture."

Ryan thought a moment, then couldn't resist. "You could come with me. I could use the advice. My wife was a great decorator, but I don't know the first thing about mixing and matching furniture."

Kristen hesitated.

"You don't have to if you don't want to," Ryan said, not wanting to make her uncomfortable. "It was just an idea."

"No, I really do want to go with you. How about Saturday morning? There are some really nice furniture stores not far from here. Or we could go to the IKEA store near the Mall of America. That's a fun place to look."

"Saturday morning's fine. I'll come get you around ten."

"Perfect," Kristen said. She smiled warmly at him. "I'm so proud of you, Ryan. I'm sure Amanda is, too. I'll see you next Saturday." She turned and pet Sam behind the ears, then waved and walked out into the night.

Ryan grinned, thinking of how much he'd enjoy spending the day with Kristen. "At least we can be friends, right, Sam?" Ryan went back to his work, no longer feeling the weight of his loss, but instead an eagerness of things to come.

* * *

The next Saturday, Ryan was at Kristen's door exactly at ten and the two headed toward the first store of the day. As they rode along, Ryan laughed. "Well, this is a first."

Kristen looked at him curiously. "What? Going furniture shopping?"

"No. This is the first time we've gone somewhere without Sam."

Kristen laughed. "I hadn't thought of that. I'll bet Sam was upset when you left today."

"I didn't tell her I was going with you," he said conspiratorially.

"Then I guess it'll have to be our little secret," Kristen whispered back.

They walked through the furniture store that Kristen had suggested, but everything was very high end and expensive.

"I think I need stuff that I won't be afraid might get ruined," he said. So they drove a short way and stopped at another place. He found a bed frame and headboard that he liked, and a dark gray sofa and chair set that was comfortable. The prices weren't bad, either.

"Let's go to IKEA and look around," he said. "That way I'll feel like I checked out all my options." They drove to the IKEA store across the street from Mall of America and walked inside.

"Sheesh. This place is big!" Ryan said. "I never expected this."

"Yeah, but you can get a lot of great ideas walking through here," Kristen said.

They started at the beginning and wandered past sofas, display kitchens, and dining rooms. They explored every room design, and lay down on a few mattresses to get a feel for them. Ryan saw a cabinet unit in black with glass doors that he really liked. He was drawn to the sleek, modern furniture, but Kristen reminded him that the guest house had a cottage feel to it.

"See. That's why I needed you along. To keep me on track."

Halfway through the store, they came to the eating area and Ryan asked if she wanted some lunch. "I'm starving," he said.

"Me, too. Let's eat."

They choose their food, paid, and walked to a back corner to sit down.

"So, we're only halfway through? Amazing," Ryan said. "I can't believe Amanda never brought me here. It seems like it would have been a decorator's heaven."

"I suppose it would be like me going to the hospital on my day off. Your wife did this for a living. I doubt she thought it would be fun for a Saturday afternoon," Kristen said, eating a french fry.

"That's probably true. So, tell me, how is Gabbie? Have you seen her lately?"

Kristen nodded. "That's sweet of you to ask. She hasn't been too well lately. They stopped her chemo treatments and are trying hard to build up her immune system. She had pneumonia last week and was in the hospital a couple of days. But she was doing better the last time I saw her. I sent her a new picture of Sam each day, and that cheered her up."

"That's nice. I'm glad Sam can help. I hope she'll be okay," Ryan said.

"I'm hoping so, too. She's been fighting this for a long time and it's wearing down her body. But she is just as determined as can be and never complains. I know a lot of adults who could learn from her," Kristen said.

"Gabbie is an inspiration. I wish she and my mother could meet. They have a lot in common. My mom's a fighter, too. I'm not sure I could be that gracious if I were that sick."

Kristen grinned. "Yeah. You'd probably be a spoiled little whiner. I can tell just by looking at you."

"Hey!" Ryan threw a french fry at her, making her laugh. She threatened to squeeze ketchup on his shirt, and he gave in. "You're probably right. I'd be a whiner," he said, laughing.

They finished walking through the store and Ryan wrote down a few things he was interested in. He loved the down comforters, so he purchased one and a duvet. But he decided he liked the bed and sofa he'd seen at the other furniture store, so they headed back there and ordered all of it.

"That furniture is going to look nice in the guest house," Kristen told him as they drove home. "You don't have such bad taste after all."

Ryan smiled and looked over at her. He wanted to tell her he had great taste in women, especially because he was falling for her. But he kept quiet. She was engaged to Bradley and was no longer available. The ring on her finger reminded him of that.

"Thanks for helping me today," Ryan said after he'd walked her to her kitchen door. "It was fun."

"Yeah, it was. I was happy to go."

"I don't suppose you'd want to go to dinner in a little bit. I mean, if you don't have plans."

Kristen shook her head. "I'm sorry, Ryan. I'm going to dinner with Bradley. Maybe another time?"

"Sure. Of course. Well, thanks again. Have a good time." Ryan waved as he walked through the bushes to his own house. *Have a good time. Yeah, right. I can't believe I said that.* Because the truth was, he really wanted her to have a terrible time with Bradley so she would see that Dr. BMW wasn't right for her.

Ryan sighed.

* * *

Kristen had so much fun furniture shopping with Ryan that she wished she hadn't made plans with Bradley. It would have been nice to have dinner with Ryan. Maybe they would have grabbed a couple of subs and eaten down by the lake. That's something Bradley would never do. He only ate at the nicest restaurants. And he would never, ever spend a Saturday wandering furniture stores. Or any stores, for that matter. She wondered how he'd furnished his condo, and realized he'd probably hired a decorator to do it. Kristen sighed. She and Bradley were so different.

Then why are you even considering marrying him?

More and more that question kept popping up in her head.

Bradley came to pick her up and drove to the country club he was a member of. The club boasted an eighteen-hole golf course, tennis courts, an Olympic-size indoor swimming pool, and handball courts. It also had a five-star restaurant that was for members only. Kristen was happy she'd worn a dress and heels because showing up here in anything less would have been a crime.

After they sat down, Kristen studied Bradley as he looked over the menu. There was no doubt that he was a good-looking man. He had Richard Gere silver hair and gorgeous blue eyes that any women would love gazing into. He kept in great shape, and always dressed to perfection. Tonight he wore casual, cream-colored trousers, a blue polo, and a brown blazer. Everything he wore was always neatly cleaned and pressed. Even when he wore jeans, he looked like he was dressed up.

"Is there something on my clothes?" Bradley asked.

Kristen blushed at having been caught staring at him. "No, no. I was just spacing out a little, I guess," she said. Quickly, she dropped her eyes to her menu.

After they'd ordered, Bradley reached across the table and touched Kristen's hand. "I'm happy to see you're wearing my ring."

Kristen looked down at the ring. She'd worn it all day while shopping with Ryan, and she wished she hadn't. She'd seen Ryan's eyes glance at it a couple of times, and his smile would fade. She felt bad about that. "I know how much you like it when I wear it," she said.

"I hope that means you're closer to saying yes."

"I'm sorry that it's taking me so long to give you an answer. Marriage is a big step for me. I have to make sure it's the right decision."

"I understand," Bradley said. "I can wait as long as you need."

Bradley asked Kristen about her day and she told him honestly that she'd been out furniture shopping with Ryan. He reacted as casually as if she'd said she'd been out all day with a girlfriend. "That must have been fun," he said.

Kristen nodded. "It was."

They made small talk about work, and Bradley even made a point to ask how Gabbie was doing. This surprised and pleased, her. Although she had a feeling that had been his motive—to show her he was interested enough in her work to remember her favorite patient.

As they were eating, Kristen remembered Ryan's comment about her moving and brought the subject up with Bradley. "If we were to get married, where would we live?"

Bradley smiled indulgently. "I was hoping you'd like to live in my condo. It's such a lovely place and a beautiful building. I have plenty of room there, and you've always said you love the master suite there."

He did have a beautiful master bedroom with a bathroom that looked like a spa. But his building was downtown where it was crowded, noisy, and impersonal. She couldn't picture herself living there after having enjoyed living in the quiet suburbs.

"I've grown to love my house and the neighborhood," she said. "I can't imagine living downtown."

Bradley considered this a moment. "You do have a nice house there, but think of how convenient my condo is. You'll be closer to work and there's a gym and swimming pool you'd be able to use. Wouldn't you like that?"

Kristen wasn't much of a swimmer. She loved walking. "I've also been considering getting a dog. We couldn't have one in your condo."

Bradley stopped eating a moment and stared at her. "A dog? I could see why you'd want one at the house, but it might be difficult in the condo. Although, some of the neighbors have small dogs. It's something we could consider later on." He reached across the table and patted her arm. "I'm open to discussing anything that would make you happy."

Kristen nodded but wasn't completely convinced. She'd felt like he was indulging the whims of a child.

When they arrived back at Kristen's house, Bradley came inside for coffee but had to leave after that.

"Sorry I can't stay," he told her, giving her a kiss on the cheek. "I have an early golf date tomorrow, and then I have to make rounds at the hospital. Would you like to meet up for an early dinner tomorrow night?"

"My sister is coming over for lunch tomorrow, so I think I'll just stay home, if you don't mind."

"That's fine. I'll call you tomorrow night." He kissed her on the lips, then left.

As Kristen watched Bradley drive away, she thought about something Ryan had said to her that night on the porch. *Why Bradley? He's too old for you, he's too full of himself, and he doesn't give you the attention you deserve.* She'd thought about that often. Why Bradley? He was handsome, he was kind, and he treated her very well. Was he too old for her? Probably. Unlike what Ryan thought, she didn't think Bradley was full of himself; he was just a very busy man who took his responsibilities seriously. And his sports, too. But what about giving her the attention she deserved? Bradley never let passion rule his decisions. If he was going to spend the night, he needed to plan for it ahead of time to fit it into his schedule. Sure, once in a while it would be nice if he wanted to make love to her at the spur of the moment. She'd like it if he'd not go golfing or play handball, or any of his other sports on a Sunday morning so they could sleep late and cuddle. But that wasn't who Bradley was. And she'd known that when she'd started dating him, so why did it bother her so much now?

Because now I've met Ryan, and he seems like he'd be a great cuddlier.

Yeah, but how many women has he cuddled with over the past couple of months?

Kristen sighed. "Maybe I'll just get a dog," she told herself as she headed upstairs to bed.

* * *

Ryan saw Bradley drive away and was happy that he hadn't stayed the night. He knew that was terrible, and it was none of his business, but he couldn't help it. He hated the thought of Bradley being close to Kristen. Bradley didn't deserve her.

Besides, what was wrong with the guy? He had a lovely, sweet fiancé and he didn't want to stay the night and wake up Sunday morning beside her. Cripes. If he were lucky enough to find a woman like Kristen, he'd spend every night lying with his arms wrapped around her. And he'd spend every morning snuggled up beside her for those last few minutes before their day began. And on the weekend? Just try to tear him away from her. If he were so lucky, which he was not.

"Maybe I had my only chance at happiness," Ryan said to Sam who was lying on the kitchen floor, watching him. Ryan looked out at the quiet night one more time, sighed, and then turned away. "Or maybe I should get my own life put back together and stop obsessing over a woman I can't have."

Chapter Eighteen

Sunday afternoon, Kristen's sister Heather showed up with subs and chips for lunch. Kristen was pouring the last of the vegetable soup she'd made into containers to refrigerate.

"The subs smell great," Kristen said, twisting the lids on the jars. She glanced out her kitchen window. It was a beautiful sunny day and she hadn't yet had a chance to go walking. "Hey, would you like to go for a walk to the park and we could eat our sandwiches there?"

Heather grimaced. "Really? A walk? How long have you known me?" She grabbed plates out of the cupboard instead and placed them on the kitchen table.

Kristen sighed. Maybe she could steal Sam later and go for a walk. But if she did, there was a good chance that Ryan would want to go, too. She hated that she was trying not to spend too much time with Ryan. She enjoyed walking with him.

They sat and ate their subs, catching up on their week. Out the window, they saw Ryan get into his car and drive off. Heather sighed dramatically.

"Tell me again why you're engaged to a one-hundred-year-old man and not dating the guy next door," Heather asked.

"He's not a hundred years old."

"Yeah, but he's halfway there. You're only thirty-two. Do you really want to take care of a drooling old man in a few years?

Wouldn't you rather *take care* of Mr. Dreamy Eyes?"

Kristen shook her head. "Mr. Dreamy Eyes has plenty of women to *take care* of his needs. I'm not interested in being one of them, thank you very much. Besides, I haven't yet accepted Bradley's proposal. I'm still thinking about it."

Heather laughed. "It's been over a month since Dr. Strangelove proposed. What do you have to think about? It's obvious you don't really want to marry him or else you'd have said yes already. Why don't you give him back his ring and move on?"

"Stop calling him all those names. His name is Bradley. And this is a big decision. Stop rushing me."

It was Heather's turn to shake her head. "You go walking with Mr. Dreamy Eyes. You share his dog. You take care of his pets while he's away. You even went furniture shopping with him. There is no way you can tell me you don't care about him."

"I do care about Ryan. As a friend. He's a good neighbor and an even better friend. That's it. That's all it can ever be."

"Then you're crazy. You have everything you could ever want right next door and you'd rather go out with the old guy. That's insane."

"Heather, when you make a life decision, you don't pick the cutest or the most popular. You pick the one who will be the most honest, loyal, and dependable. And that's why I'm considering Bradley's proposal. He's all those things."

Heather snorted. "So is a dog. Get one of those instead and save yourself from a lifetime of misery."

Kristen rolled her eyes as she picked up her plate and walked over to the sink. Her baby sister didn't understand. She still believed in true love and soul mates. Kristen no longer believed in those things. She wasn't going to marry for the wrong reasons the second time around. This time, she'd make sure her choice was the right one. The one that wasn't going to hurt her in the end. But as she gazed out the window toward Ryan's house, she couldn't help but wish he'd been that guy.

* * *

The next couple of weeks went by quickly for Kristen. Gabbie came down with pneumonia again and stayed several days in the hospital. Gabbie had lost more weight and was so pale and worn down, it worried Kristen. She spent as much time as possible with her while she was working and stayed late two evenings to sit with Gabbie while her mother went home to tend to her sister. Kristen saw the strain on Gabbie's mother's face as well, and wanted to do whatever she could to make her life easier. Kristen didn't usually become this involved with her patients, but Gabbie was different. Kristen couldn't have gone home and forgotten about her even if she'd tried. The sweet, soulful girl had become too important to her.

Gabbie was sent home on the weekend, still tired and worn, but her lungs were clear again. Kristen tried not to worry about her as she went through her usual routine. Ryan stopped by on Sunday and asked if she'd be able to care for the animals during the week while he was away at a sales training meeting. Kristen was only too happy to say yes. She looked forward to having Sam for company and watching the two cats. She'd grown fond of the chubby pair and she adored Sam.

Kristen made excuses to Bradley when he'd suggest a night out. She knew she wasn't being fair to Bradley, but she needed some time to herself to sort out her feelings. She knew deep down in her heart that she didn't truly love him, and he'd never professed his love for her, either. He'd said that he had a "deep affection" for her. That they'd have a wonderful life together. Yes, Bradley could provide a lovely life for her, but what about love? What about passion?

"What about children?" Kristen said aloud one evening to Sam as they sat in the living room sharing a cookie and watching television.

Sam looked up at her curiously.

"Bradley wouldn't want children. Not at his age. But I do." She looked down into Sam's amber eyes. "Heck, he doesn't even want a dog. How can I live without a dog?"

Sam smiled and licked her lips, clearly hoping for another bite of cookie.

Kristen laughed and gave her the last piece.

"I don't know, Sam. I just don't know. Bradley has everything to offer, but nothing that I want." She shook her head. "Maybe that's my answer right there." She smiled down at Sam. "You know, you're a good listener. I'm glad you're here with me tonight."

Sam gave her a grin.

Kristen thought about Ryan and the big changes he was making in his life. Packing up the cottage had to have been difficult for him. And then, while she was over at his place feeding the cats, she'd noticed that he'd put away some of the pictures of Amanda. Only two sat on the hutch now, and the ones in the hallway were gone.

"Probably to impress Christy or Nichole, or some other woman," Kristen told Sam. "I know it's good for him to finally move on, but I doubt any of the women he's dating appreciate what he's doing for them. Only I understand how hard it was for him to put away his memories of Amanda." She looked down at Sam and ran her hand over the dog's silky fur. "And you, Sam. You understand, too."

A week after Ryan came home from his trip, Kristen noticed he was working in the cottage again. It was late afternoon on the

Fourth of July and Kristen had declined an invitation from Bradley to attend the country club's annual party and one from her sister to go with her friends to a local carnival and fireworks. Kristen hadn't felt in the holiday mood and being in a place crowded with people sounded exhausting. Instead, she cleaned her house and started preparing her soup for the week. This week's choice was tomato bisque. She gathered all the ingredients and would chop, mix, cook, and puree it all tomorrow.

Once she saw Ryan outside, though, she became curious about how the cottage was coming along. It was hot and sticky outside—a typical July day— when Kristen walked over to Ryan's. Sam greeted her at the door when she peeked inside. "Hi. I saw you were working out here so I had to come snoop."

Ryan turned and smiled at her. "Come on in. The furniture came this week so I'm setting it up."

Kristen stepped inside and looked around. Ryan had painted a fresh coat of creamy white on the walls, making it look clean and crisp. The bed was set up, and he'd placed the new comforter and pillows on it. The dark gray fabric-tufted headboard looked nice against the cream-colored walls and the gray sofa and chair he'd purchased fit in perfectly. He'd also set up a wall cabinet for books and knick-knacks. It was an antique white with wicker baskets on the bottom shelf.

"I went back to IKEA and bought the shelf unit I liked," Ryan said. "But I bought the antique white instead of the black. I think it looks nice in here."

"It does," Kristen told him. "You've done a great job. It's very cozy."

"Thanks. Now I have to decide on colors for the bathroom. I'd love your help some weekend if you have the time."

"Sure," Kristen said.

Ryan stared at her a moment, looking as if he wanted to say something.

"What's wrong?" Kristen asked, becoming self-conscious from his gaze.

"Nothing. I was just wondering why you aren't out celebrating the fourth with Bradley."

"He asked me to his country club's party, but I didn't really feel like being in a crowd today," she said.

Ryan whistled softly. "Country club party, huh? Sounds swanky. You mean you don't want to hob nob with the upper crust?"

"Very funny. I'm just not one for parties. I had a long week and I'm tired. Besides, who are you to talk? You're not out celebrating with one of your many girlfriends."

Ryan snorted. "One of my many girlfriends? No, I wanted a quiet weekend, too. I'd rather do this than go out partying."

They both stood there, silent a moment, until Kristen started feeling awkward about being there. "Well, I should let you get back to work. I'll see you around." She turned to leave but stopped when Ryan called her name.

"Kristen? Since we're both not doing anything today, would you like to grab a bite to eat? I'm done here and I'm getting kind of hungry."

Kristen hesitated. She wasn't sure if it was a good idea for her and Ryan to spend time together. But going for dinner did sound good. After all, it was just dinner. "Sure. Why not? That sounds good."

"Great. I'll change out of my dirty clothes and come get you in a few minutes, okay?"

Kristen nodded. She patted Sam on the head and then headed back over to her place. *It's only dinner. Nothing special.*

Then why am I so excited about going?

* * *

Ryan hurried inside, washed up, and changed into a clean shirt and jeans. His mood had lifted considerably the moment Kristen had entered the cottage. She wasn't out with Bradley, so that was one reason he was so happy. And now she was going to dinner with him. He knew it didn't mean anything—it was just a friendly dinner—but it still made him happy enough to hum a favorite song as he fed Sam and the cats before heading over to Kristen's.

They drove a short distance to a small café that Ryan sometimes ate at. It wasn't fancy, but they had great burgers and friendly service. It wasn't very busy, so they chose a booth in the back corner and the waitress handed them their menus and left them to decide.

"You know all these out of the way places around here," Kristen said, looking around. "This reminds me of an old diner, but it's clean and kept up. It's a nice change from the chain restaurants."

"Yeah, I like it here. When I crave a burger, I come here. I never feel self-conscious about dining alone in here like I would in other restaurants."

Kristen raised her eyebrows. "You dine alone? I can't imagine with all the women you're seeing that you have to do that."

Ryan frowned. "Who are all these women you have me dating? I don't go out much."

"Well, there's Nichole and that woman, Christy. I'm sure there are several others I've never met. Don't you go out to bars on weekends to meet women?"

Ryan laughed. "Who do you think I am? Hugh Hefner? Believe me, there isn't a mansion full of eager women waiting for me each weekend. And I rarely go out anymore."

Kristen looked like she was about to reply when the waitress came. They both ordered cheeseburgers, fries, and Cokes. After she left, Ryan asked Kristen how Gabbie was doing, and that brought a worried frown to her face.

"She was back in the hospital with pneumonia the week before last, and I was very worried about her. She's growing weaker, and there's nothing that can be done. Her immune system just can't fight anything anymore. She's home now, and I hope she can grow stronger."

"You really care about her, don't you? I can understand why. She's such a special girl. I hope she feels better soon."

Kristen nodded. "It's hard. I'm not supposed to get this close with my patients, but she's a different case. And it's so sweet of you to always ask about her. I'm hoping she'll feel better so we can bring Sam for a visit again, if you don't mind. Sam would help lift her spirits."

Ryan liked how Kristen had said *we* can bring Sam for a visit. "I'd love to do that. Anytime, just let me know and Sam and I'll be there."

Their food came and they dug in. After a time, Kristen asked about Ryan's mother.

"She's doing pretty good, considering. She finished her fifth week of chemo this week and has one more to go. She doesn't complain, but my dad says she's been pretty sick with the chemo this time around. They're hoping she won't have to go through radiation after this, but if it's necessary, she will. My mom is a tough cookie when she wants to be."

"I'd love to meet her someday. She sounds like my kind of woman."

Ryan smiled. "She'd like that. She already likes you."

"Really? Why is that?" Kristen looked up, surprised.

"I've told her a little about you, like how you walk Sam and watch my animals for me. She's very impressed by you because of your job and that you love animals."

"Wow. That's kind of neat. Now I really want to meet her."

They sat in the booth and talked long after they'd finished

their burgers. The waitress brought refills on their sodas, and they felt guilty for staying so long, so they ordered a piece of chocolate fudge cake and shared it. Finally, Ryan looked at his phone and saw it was almost eight-thirty.

"Have we really been here that long?" he asked. "No wonder the waitress has finally given up on us."

"We should go," Kristen said. "It's been fun talking, but it's getting late."

Ryan glanced outside. It was still light out and would be until ten. "Say? We still have time to drive down to the river and watch the fireworks. They don't start until after ten. I know of a great place by the Stone Arch Bridge where we can see them."

"You want to drive in holiday traffic all the way downtown to see the fireworks? Isn't that a little crazy?"

Ryan shrugged. "I haven't gone to watch them since Amanda died. It might be fun. Come on, let's go."

Kristen grinned. "Sure. Why not? I never do anything spontaneous anymore."

They headed outside to the car. The air was cooling off, and the humidity had lessened. Ryan turned the car toward Highway 35W and drove to downtown Minneapolis.

They exited a while later and drove around until they found a parking spot several blocks away. Dusk was settling in and the air had cooled considerably. Kristen shivered.

"Wait a second," Ryan said, going to the back of his car. He pulled something out and came back to Kristen. "I always keep a jacket and sweatshirt in my car. If you don't mind it being too big, you can wear this." He handed her a Minnesota Vikings sweatshirt.

"Thanks, I think I'd be chilled with only this T-shirt on." She slipped it over her head. It smelled like fabric softener and Ryan's spicy cologne. "So, you're a Vikings fan, even though you're from Iowa."

Ryan chuckled. "Iowa doesn't have a team and since I live here, I'd better root for the Vikings. Don't tell me you're a Cheesehead!"

"I don't follow sports. But if I did, I'd be a Vikings fan. I like the color purple." Kristen laughed as Ryan rolled his eyes.

They walked along and finally came to a grassy section that had a view of the beautiful Stone Arch Bridge over the Mississippi River which weaved itself through downtown Minneapolis. It was getting darker, but the city lights reflecting off the water helped to light up the area. Many other people were there, too, with blankets or chairs to sit on. Ryan found an open spot and laid down his jacket so they could sit on it.

"Such a gentleman," Kristen teased as she sat down.

"Well, you know I've had so much practice with all those women I'm seeing," he said with a wink.

Kristen laughed.

As darkness settled around them the audience began to quiet down in anticipation of the fireworks show. Soon, the night sky lit up with the first of many sunbursts of color as the fireworks exploded high above.

Ryan and Kristen sat close together so they'd both fit on the jacket. As the crowd oohed and aahed over the fireworks display, Ryan turned to look at Kristen. Her full attention was on the show in the sky, and he smiled at the excitement he saw on her face. She'd pulled her hair out of its ponytail earlier because of the cool evening and it hung down past her shoulders. He wanted nothing more than to run his fingers through her hair and feel its silkiness. She turned then, catching him staring at her, and smiled up at him warmly, her eyes reflecting the lights in the sky. They gazed into each other's eyes and before Ryan realized what he was doing, he dropped his lips to hers.

Chapter Nineteen

Kristen responded to Ryan's kiss with a fervor that surprised even her. She knew she should pull away and stop him, but her body had other ideas. She lifted her arms around his neck and pulled him to her, savoring his delicious kiss. Their tongues met and teased, and Kristen felt chills tingle down her spine. He reached around her, his hand lingering at the base of her neck. Her body grew warm with delight at his touch, and as the kiss deepened, so did her desire for him. When he finally pulled away and looked down into her eyes, she wished he hadn't stopped.

And that was when she thought of Bradley.

For a moment, it looked like Ryan was going to say something to her, but she shook her head slightly and turned away, staring up at the fireworks again. She didn't want to hear him apologize for kissing her. Or worse yet, confusing her even more than she already was by proclaiming to have feelings for her. *It's best if we don't say anything,* she thought. He still had his arm around her and she didn't try to push it away. She savored the feel of him holding her close.

When the fireworks ended, everyone stood up and packed their things away to leave. Ryan picked up his jacket and shook it out, then put it on. The night was growing colder and they had a long walk back to the car. Kristen didn't look at him the entire time they walked because she was afraid if she did, she'd fall back under his spell and wouldn't be able to stop herself with just a kiss.

They drove home in silence. Kristen could tell that Ryan wanted to talk, but she turned away every time she thought he might say something. She couldn't face reality right now. She wanted to remember the warmth of his lips on hers, the feel of his hand on her neck. Words would only ruin the memory. Soon enough, she'd have to think about the ramifications of her feelings for Ryan when she was supposed to be considering Bradley's proposal.

Once they pulled into Ryan's driveway, Kristen sprang out of the car and hurried to her house. Ryan was close behind. When she reached her door, she could no longer ignore him. He was on the step below her, so near she could feel the heat of his body. She turned and gazed into his eyes. What she saw in them startled her. He was looking at her with such tenderness, such warmth, it unnerved her.

"Please don't be angry at me," he said softly. "I hadn't planned on kissing you. But like before, I'm not sorry. I care deeply for you, Kristen. You must know that."

Kristen dropped her eyes as her heart pounded. She shook her head slowly. "I can't do this, Ryan. I'm sorry." She reached up and pulled him close, hugging him tightly. "I'm sorry," she whispered into his ear. Then she turned and fled into her house, closing the door behind her as tears fell down her cheeks.

Kristen ran upstairs to her bed and dropped on it. Hot tears spilled from her eyes. Once again, Ryan had made her cry, and it both hurt her and angered her. She wasn't angry at Ryan; she was angry with herself. How could she have let herself develop feelings for Ryan? She'd been so careful these past few weeks to make it clear they were just friends. But it was hard. He was kind and caring, he loved animals, and he was so damned sweet, always asking about Gabbie. How could she not fall for a guy like him?

Because guys like him are easy to fall for. He knows how to pull women in with those warm, chocolate-brown eyes.

Kristen pulled herself up and sat back against her pillows, wiping her eyes. She realized she was still wearing Ryan's sweatshirt, and despite herself, she hugged it close around her, feeling its cozy warmth and inhaling his cologne. It was hard for her to believe that Ryan was a player. He'd been nothing but kind to her, except when he talked about Bradley, alias Mr. BMW. And he'd always seemed so sincere, especially about his feelings for his wife. There was no way he could fake that. She had to accept that he was a good guy.

But that would make my life more complicated.

Bradley didn't complicate her life. She knew exactly what he wanted. She believed he'd be good to her and they would have a great companionship.

But is that all I want?

Kristen let her thoughts wander to both times that Ryan had kissed her. Each time, her body had reacted with such intensity, it surprised her. He was a great kisser. And he brought out the passion in her that Bradley didn't. But with Bradley, she would have a secure relationship. Would she have that with Ryan? Could he ever love another woman as he had his wife? And what about the other women? Could she forget that he'd been dating Nichole and Christy and God knows who else? Her ex-husband had cheated on her. She couldn't risk that heartbreak again.

"When did my life get so complicated?"

Kristen pulled back the covers and crawled into bed still wearing Ryan's sweatshirt. She didn't want to take it off. Tomorrow, she'd wash it and give it back. Tonight, she'd enjoy the feel of him around her before returning to the reality of her life.

* * *

Ryan couldn't believe he'd done it again. By drawing Kristen closer he'd actually pushed her farther away. Now, she'd back away from him even more, and he'd probably never see her again. All because he couldn't stop from kissing her.

But he sure did enjoy kissing her.

The cats and Sam were waiting anxiously for him at the kitchen door when he came inside. He fed them a late dinner and then headed upstairs to his bedroom. Sam soon appeared and sat happily beside the bed as Ryan undressed and crawled under the blankets.

"I messed up tonight, girl," Ryan told Sam as he stared into her big, amber eyes. "I couldn't help it, though. If you'd been there, you'd know what I mean."

Ryan had never felt as close to anyone, other than Amanda, as he'd felt toward Kristen. He just had to kiss her. It seemed like the most natural thing to do at the time.

"And now I've ruined everything again," he said sadly. "Just when she started trusting me after the last kiss, I went and did it again." But would he take it back if he could?

No. I'm falling in love with her.

For the first time since losing his wife, Ryan felt a true, deep love for someone else. He couldn't deny it any longer. He adored everything about Kristen, from her easygoing nature to her deep concern for her patients and how warm and caring she was. Kristen was genuine. She was the real deal. There was nothing phony about her in any way.

"And she'll probably never talk to me again," Ryan said to Sam.

Ryan knew he couldn't compete with Dr. BMW. He knew Kristen well enough to know that she didn't care about his money or fancy toys. She was too down-to-earth to marry a man for his money. He must have something else that made her love him. He must be a very special person, because Kristen wouldn't marry someone unless they were. And that left him out completely. Obviously, Dr. BMW had something that Ryan didn't.

"Besides charm, good looks, and money," Ryan said. "None of which I have."

Ryan turned out his light and sunk deeper into bed. The cats had crawled up into their spots and Sam had curled up on her pillow. *Maybe Kristen will give me one more chance to be just friends.* He hoped she would. Because if he wasn't allowed to love her, at least he could be around her once in a while. That was the best he could do.

* * *

Over the next two weeks, Kristen managed to avoid both Ryan and Bradley. She'd meant to return Ryan's sweatshirt, but it still sat on the kitchen table, washed and folded neatly. Every time she looked at it, it reminded her of that night and she relived how sweet his kiss had felt on her lips. If she really wanted to be rid of that memory, she'd have used her key to set the sweatshirt in his house long ago. But she couldn't part with it—the sweatshirt or the memory.

And that led to her confusion about Bradley.

He'd called several times to go out, and each time she'd made up an excuse not to see him. She couldn't go out with him when she was confused about another man. But she also knew it wasn't fair to Bradley. He was still waiting for an answer to his proposal, and she couldn't give it to him. It frustrated her how confusing her life had become. So she avoided both men and put her energy into her work instead.

On a stormy Friday evening, Gabbie was admitted into the hospital. She'd passed out at home, and her mother had been frantic. Gabbie's heart rate was weak, and she still hadn't regained her strength since her bout with pneumonia. Her breathing was shallow, causing concern that fluid may have entered her lungs.

Kristen helped Gabbie get settled into her bed, hooked up the heart monitor, and placed the oxygen tube under her nose. The doctor ordered an X-ray for her lungs, and after that came back, Kristen gave Gabbie medicine through her chemo-port as ordered by her doctor to clear her lungs. Gabbie's mother was with the doctor in the hall, so as Kristen worked, she kept up a steady flow of conversation with Gabbie to take her mind off of how poorly she felt. Gabbie's answers were mostly nods or shakes of her head, and an occasional smile since she was too weak to talk. Once Kristen was done, she sat down beside Gabbie and showed her the most recent photo of Sam that she'd taken with her phone. This brought a sweet smile to Gabbie's face.

"As soon as you're feeling better, Ryan said we could bring Sam over for a visit," Kristen told her, even though she wasn't sure the offer was still open. Knowing how Ryan felt about Gabbie, though, Kristen was confident he'd still do it for her. "So you need to get well soon, okay?"

Gabbie nodded. She lifted a hand and motioned for Kristen to come nearer. Kristen bent down closer to Gabbie.

"He's a nice man," Gabbie whispered. "You should keep him."

Kristen pulled away and looked down into Gabbie's brown eyes. In them, she saw what she'd been refusing to see for months. Gabbie was worn out. She was tired from five long years of treatments for a cancer that wouldn't go away. Gabbie knew, just as Kristen did, that she was nearing the end. And still, even in her own pain, she was worried about Kristen's happiness. It was so like Gabbie. She didn't have to go to Heaven to become an angel: she was already one on earth.

Kristen reached down and gently brushed the back of her hand along Gabbie's smooth cheek. "You're right. He is a nice man," she said softly.

"Keep him. And Sam, too," Gabbie said so quietly that Kristen could barely hear her.

"You rest now," Kristen told her, holding back tears. She wanted to assure the young girl that she was going to be fine and she'd live a long, happy life. But Gabbie couldn't be fooled that easily. She was a smart girl and she'd see right through Kristen's false hope.

Gabbie nodded and closed her eyes.

Kristen stood up and walked to the door. She took a deep breath to regain her composure, then stepped out into the hall where Lisa was, talking with Gabbie's doctor. Tears pooled in the woman's eyes, and the doctor reached out and gently patted her shoulder. Kristen straightened her shoulders, determined to be strong for Gabbie's mother.

After the doctor walked away, Kristen went up to Lisa and wrapped her arm around her shoulders. "I'll sit with you, if you'd like," she said, and Lisa nodded as she wiped the tears from her eyes. Together, they turned and entered Gabbie's room.

Chapter Twenty

Ryan sat on his sofa eating chips and watching a movie on television. Sam lay on the floor below him, hoping to catch the crumbs. It was late on a Friday night, and Ryan had nowhere to go and no one to be with. A powerful thunderstorm had been raging all evening and rain pelted down noisily on the roof. It was nice to be safely inside, out of the rain, but it would have been nicer if someone was snuggled up next to him.

The movie he was watching didn't help make him feel any better. He could have chosen to watch anything—an action movie, a thriller, even a comedy. Instead, he'd stopped on the romance movie *Kate & Leopold,* one of his wife's favorites. He watched as Meg Ryan fell in love with Hugh Jackman, a man who'd been accidently brought from the past to the present.

"Hmm. Maybe the only way to find a woman who enjoys romance is to time travel. I certainly can't find one here," Ryan told Sam. Sam looked up at him. "Yeah, I get it, girl. I'm also no Hugh Jackman." *Or no Dr. BMW.*

Someone knocked on his front door, startling Ryan. "What the…" He looked at the clock on the DVR—eleven p.m. "Who's knocking on my door at this time of night?"

Ryan glanced out the peep hole. He opened the door and there, standing on his porch, was Nichole.

"Hey there. Aren't you going to let a girl in? It's pouring out here."

Ryan quickly unlocked the screen door and Nichole sauntered in. He turned and stared at her. She'd already taken off her rain jacket and was wearing a tight black dress and tall heels, and she had a streak of fluorescent green in her hair.

"What are you doing here?" Ryan asked, stunned that she'd showed up at his door. "I haven't seen you in weeks."

Nichole glanced around the living room. "That's right. I haven't seen you out in weeks and I was wondering what you're up to." Her eyes dropped onto the television and bag of chips. "A chick flick and junk food? It looks like I got here in the nick of time." She smiled and walked up to Ryan, running her hand over his chest and up around his neck. Pulling him to her, she kissed him deeply, before finally pulling away.

Ryan felt dazed after the kiss. "Uh, would you like a glass of wine or something?"

Nichole laughed. "No, I'm fine." She gently rubbed a hand up and down his chest. It felt warm even through his T-shirt. "Everything I want is right here." She reached up to kiss him again, but was stopped by a pounding on the kitchen door.

Ryan pulled away and hurried to the kitchen. Only one person he knew would use the kitchen door, and that was Kristen.

He pulled it open and she came running inside, dripping wet, still wearing her scrubs. She stopped in front of Ryan and looked up at him with tears streaming down her face.

"Gabbie's gone. She died tonight. Oh, Ryan, she's gone." More tears spilled and Ryan reached for her, pulling her close.

Ryan's heart lurched. "Oh, Kristen. I'm sorry. I'm so, so sorry."

Sam came running into the kitchen and whined, visibly upset by Kristen's tears. She sat down next to Kristen's leg.

Kristen pulled away a moment, then backed up, her eyes widening as she stared over Ryan's shoulder. "I'm so sorry," she said hoarsely. "I didn't realize anyone else was here."

Ryan frowned, then remembered that Nichole was in the living room behind him. He turned to see a confused look on Nichole's face. He turned back to Kristen. "No, no. It's okay. Gabbie's the important one now."

But Kristen was backing away. "I'm so sorry," she said, placing her hands over her mouth. "I shouldn't have bothered you. I'm sorry." Before Ryan could say another word, Kristen turned and ran out the kitchen door.

Ryan wanted to bolt after her, but he had Nichole to take care of first. "Sam, follow her. Go on," he said, waving a hand toward Kristen's fleeing figure. Sam didn't need to be told twice. She ran out into the rain after Kristen.

Ryan walked back into the living room to Nichole. "I'm sorry. Something very important has come up. A little girl Kristen and I both knew has passed away. I should be with Kristen right now."

"Of course," Nichole said, looking stunned. "You should be with her. I'm sorry about your friend."

Ryan came up to Nichole and hugged her. "Thanks," he said softly. He helped her on with her coat and offered to walk her to her car.

"Don't be silly," Nichole said, sounding more like her usual self. "You go make sure Kristen is okay. I'll see you around."

Ryan nodded and watched as Nichole ran through the rain to her car. Once she was safely inside, he waved and then closed and locked the front door. He hurriedly walked into his kitchen, threw on a jacket that was hung over a kitchen chair, and then headed out the kitchen door. He was over at Kristen's in a flash, not even bothering to knock. He walked inside and there, kneeling on the kitchen floor in a puddle of water, was Kristen, sobbing and hugging Sam close.

Ryan's heart went out to her, but he forced himself to be the strong one. He ran through the house to the bathroom and found a towel, then hurried back to Kristen. He reached out and helped her up, wrapped the towel around her shoulders, then pulled her into his arms.

"I'm so sorry, Kristen. Gabbie will be missed terribly," he said softly into her ear. He held her tightly while she cried on his shoulder, rubbing her back gently with one hand. After a time, Kristen pulled back and looked up into Ryan's eyes.

"It all happened so quickly. She was there, and then she was gone. No one expected her to go so soon," she said, tears still falling.

"I'm so, so sorry, Kristen," Ryan said again, at a loss as to what else to say. His heart was also broken over Gabbie's loss, and he'd only met her once. He knew he couldn't say anything that would make Kristen feel better right now.

She dropped her head on his shoulder and he gently rocked her in his arms. After a time, Ryan felt her shiver and he pulled back. "You need to get out of those wet clothes," he said gently.

Kristen sniffed and nodded, and he placed his arm around her waist and led her upstairs and to her bedroom. Sam followed, looking worried about Kristen.

"I'll let you change," Ryan said, tucking a stray strand of wet hair behind her ear with his finger. "Can I make you a cup of tea or something to warm you up?"

"Hot chocolate would be nice," she said, her voice small.

Ryan smiled. "Hot chocolate it is. I'll be back in a few minutes."

Ryan ran down the stairs and rummaged through the cabinets. He found a few packets of instant hot chocolate and set to work boiling water. By the time he returned upstairs with a mug of hot chocolate, Kristen had changed into sweats and was lying in bed with Sam on the floor, keeping watch over her.

Ryan handed her the mug and sat down on the side of the

bed. "Feeling better?"

Kristen nodded. She wrapped her hands around the mug and took a sip of the hot chocolate. "Thank you. I'm so sorry I'm being such a baby. I just loved Gabbie so much. It was hard watching her go."

"No apologies are necessary," Ryan told her. "Gabbie was a special girl. I can only imagine how hard it was for you to be there when she left this world."

"I sat with her mother long after my shift was over. There was something in Gabbie's eyes that told me she wouldn't be with us long. And her doctor prepared us for the worst. No one had expected to lose her so soon, though. But the poor girl had fought so long and hard, and I think her body just couldn't fight it anymore. Her heart just gave out. When she took her last breath, I wanted to fall to pieces, right then and there. But I was strong for her mother. By the time I got home, I fell apart."

"That was so kind of you to be there for Gabbie's mother. And for Gabbie. You're a good person, Kristen. You have a right to fall to pieces every so often."

Kristen's eyelids grew heavy so Ryan took her drink from her and set it on the nightstand. "Why don't you get some sleep. I'll leave Sam with you tonight, and check on you in the morning, okay?"

Kristen slid down in bed and Ryan folded the covers up around her. He bent down and placed a soft kiss on her cheek. "Goodnight," he whispered. He patted Sam's head, then turned to leave.

"Please stay," Kristen said softly.

Ryan turned around and looked at her, surprised.

"I don't want to be alone."

Ryan nodded and walked around the bed. He slipped off his shoes and lay down on top of the covers. Kristen had turned onto her right side, and she reached her arm back toward Ryan.

He rolled over next to her, curling his body around hers and tucking his arm around her.

"Goodnight," he whispered.

Kristen snuggled in closer. "Thank you, Ryan," she said. "Gabbie was right. You are a nice man."

Ryan lay there, feeling the warmth of Kristen in his arms even through the blankets. The rain had settled into a soft patter on the roof, a gentle lullaby. He closed his eyes and let the rain sing him to sleep.

* * *

Kristen awoke the next morning to the sun shining through the edges of her curtains. She lay there a minute, slowly remembering yesterday and last night. Had she dreamt she'd run over to Ryan's place and that he'd come over here to take care of her? Had she dreamt asking him to stay and feeling his strong arms around her all night? She stirred and was surprised when a furry face with big amber eyes popped up from the floor and stared at her.

Kristen laughed. "Good morning, Sam. At least I know I didn't dream you up." Kristen turned slowly and looked behind her, and was disappointed Ryan wasn't there. A piece of paper lay on the pillow instead, so she lifted it up and read it.

Went to the house to feed the cats and then off to pick up some fresh muffins from the diner. Be back soon. Ryan.

Kristen smiled. She hadn't dreamt that Ryan had stayed the night.

She got up and went into the bathroom. She looked a mess. Mascara was streaked down her cheeks and her hair was smashed to her head.

"I'll be out in a minute, girl," she told Sam and then started the shower and got inside. As the warm water fell over her, her thoughts wandered back to yesterday. Gabbie was gone. She'd known Gabbie for five years, since the first time she came in after her diagnosis for chemo treatments. She'd just turned seven, but there was something so serene about her that had drawn Kristen in immediately. Through the years, Kristen had seen Gabbie in good times and bad, and although Kristen knew the statistics of children with leukemia, she'd always hoped that Gabbie would be the one to beat the odds. Now she was gone.

Kristen thought about last night and the tender way Ryan had cared for her after she'd fallen to pieces. No one had ever taken care of her like that. The way he'd wrapped her in the towel to warm her and then made her hot chocolate. Then he'd stayed the night, chastely lying on top of the covers, holding her in his arms.

Keep him. Those were Gabbie's last words to Kristen. But how could she keep Ryan when he wasn't hers?

One thing was for certain—she misjudged him. He wasn't a player or a womanizer. He was the real deal. A good man with a good heart.

Keep him.

Unfortunately, Ryan belonged to someone else. Nichole had been at his place last night. Ryan was still seeing her. And Kristen wasn't free, either. She still had Bradley's proposal to consider. But despite all of Bradley's attributes, he was no Ryan. Not by a longshot. When she'd called Bradley last night before heading home and told him about Gabbie's death, he'd only reminded her she shouldn't have become close to her patient. He hadn't offered to come and stay with her. He hadn't offered to comfort her. He was definitely not like Ryan.

Kristen sighed. The next few days were going to be tough. She would call Gabbie's mom today to check on her and then there would be the funeral. It would be hard saying goodbye again to the sweet, soulful girl who lit up a room just by being in it.

* * *

Ryan ran over to his house and quickly fed the cats, then showered and changed clothes. He picked up a bowl and a can of food for Sam, and then hopped in his car to drive to the diner. He wanted to bring Kristen fresh muffins for breakfast. He'd do anything to bring a smile to her face after the devastating news last night.

He thought back to the night before, lying in bed with Kristen and holding her tight. He knew he was just there to bring her comfort, and he was happy he could do that for her. But he also enjoyed holding her as he slept. It felt so right. Except for the fact that she wasn't his.

Ryan sighed.

He headed back to Kristen's house and quietly let himself in. She'd been sleeping so soundly that he hadn't wanted to wake her. She needed her sleep after the emotionally draining day she'd had. He knew she'd have some tough days ahead, too, and wanted to make things as easy for her as possible.

Walking upstairs with the box of muffins, he stepped into her bedroom and saw Sam on the floor, but the bed was empty. He turned toward the bathroom and that's when he realized that the door was open and the shower was running. Through the steamy glass shower door, he could see the outline of her body as she ran her hands through her hair. Ryan stood there, mesmerized. He couldn't see details, just her curvy outline. It took him a second to realize he was watching her shower, and how inappropriate that was.

Sheesh. What's wrong with me? It's Kristen.

Ryan backed up, feeling guilty. He glanced over at Sam, who shot him a curious look. "Hey, I wasn't *trying* to look," he whispered to Sam. Sam just laid her head back down.

Ryan decided he should make it known he was there before Kristen came out of the bathroom. "I'm back!" he yelled loud enough so she could hear over the water. "I brought muffins."

"Great!" she yelled back, as if it were the most natural thing in the world for Ryan to be in her bedroom. "I'll be out in a few minutes. Would you make some coffee?"

"I'll go make it now." He waved at Sam to follow him so he could feed her and then headed down the stairs.

Kristen came downstairs a little while later wearing a T-shirt and shorts and her wet hair pulled up with a clip. She looked refreshed, but her expression was serious. "I just spoke with Gabbie's mom. She's not doing so well. I think I'll go over there today and see what I can do."

"I'm sure she'll appreciate that," Ryan said. "Sit down first and I'll pour you some coffee. Do you use cream or sugar?"

"No, just black." Kristen sat at the table as Ryan poured her coffee and brought it to her. Then he found plates and napkins and brought them over to the table, as well. He opened the box in the center of the table.

"Blueberry or apple cinnamon?" he asked.

Kristen stared at him.

"What? Is something wrong?"

"No one has ever waited on me before," she said.

"Ever?"

Kristen accepted the muffin and shrugged. "My mother, but that's about it. I've been doing for others for so long that I guess I forgot what it was like to be waited on. It's nice."

Ryan smiled. "You deserve it. I hope Bradley knows that."

Kristen focused on the muffin and took a sip of coffee. Finally, she looked up at Ryan again. "Thank you for being so kind last night. I don't usually fall apart. But you were so good to me. And I'm sorry I ruined your date with Nichole. I really didn't mean to. I only came over to tell you about Gabbie."

"I was happy to take care of you," Ryan said gently, catching her eyes with his. "And don't worry about Nichole. It wasn't a date. She came over on her own, only a few minutes before you came in. It was strange, too, because I haven't seen her in weeks and then she just showed up late at night."

Kristen stared at him and then a laugh escaped her lips. "You mean it was a booty call?"

Ryan's eyes grew wide. "No. Was it? Oh, my God. I've never had a booty call before. I didn't even know it was one."

Kristen broke out laughing. "You know, I had you pegged as the playboy type, but you can't be. You don't even know a booty call when it's staring you in the face."

Ryan laughed too. It seemed ridiculous. A booty call, at his age.

"Lisa did say that the funeral is planned for Monday."

Ryan nodded. "Would you like me to go with you?"

Kristen sat there a moment, as if considering his offer. Ryan was afraid she'd want Bradley to go with her instead. Either way, he would attend. He hadn't known Gabbie long, but he adored her just the same.

"I'd like that. Thank you, Ryan."

"I'm happy to do it," he said.

They both sat and ate while Sam watched them from her spot on the floor. Ryan thought the three of them made a nice family scene. Unfortunately, they weren't a family.

Chapter Twenty-One

Attending any funeral is sad, but when it's a child's funeral, it's even more heartbreaking. Ryan did his best to stay strong for Kristen and be a shoulder she could lean on, but it was hard. Watching Gabbie's family mourn her loss nearly brought him to tears several times. And poor Kristen. She was just as devastated. Even though Ryan could tell she was trying to hold back the bulk of her emotion, she still had tears falling after every Bible passage or song. Ryan wrapped his arm around her often so she could pull strength from him. It was all he could offer at a time when everyone was breaking down with sorrow.

After the funeral, Gabbie's mother came up to them and thanked Kristen for all she'd done for Gabbie over the years.

"You were more than a nurse to her. I hope you know that. You were her friend. And my friend, too. Thank you for making these years easier for Gabbie."

Kristen nodded. "It was easy to do. Gabbie was special. I couldn't help but fall in love with her."

Lisa turned to Ryan. "And thank you for bringing Sam to her birthday party. She so adored that dog, above all others. She spoke of Sam often, and pictures of Sam brought smiles to her face even when she was hurting."

Ryan's heart warmed. How thoughtful it was of this woman, who'd just lost her daughter, to thank him. "I was happy to do it. As Kristen said, Gabbie was special."

As Lisa walked away to greet other guests, Kristen turned to Ryan. "I hadn't told you this but the last thing Gabbie said to me was that you were a nice man. And she was right. You are."

Shivers ran through Ryan. He reached out and pulled Kristen close, holding her for a long time. He remembered how she'd said the same thing to him that night after Gabbie died. He felt honored that Gabbie thought of him that way. He'd remember that, and her, for the rest of his life.

After Ryan drove Kristen home, he walked her to her kitchen door. It was late afternoon and the day was cloudy and cool, not typical for July. They stood there in silence, neither knowing what else to say. What was there to say when you'd just witnessed such a heart-wrenching event? Finally, Kristen broke the silence.

"Thank you, Ryan. For caring so much for Gabbie. For being so kind to me. For everything."

Ryan shook his head. "No, Kristen. Thank you."

Kristen's eyebrows rose. "For what?"

"For giving me the opportunity to meet Gabbie. She was so special, and I feel honored to have known her. And for being such a warm, caring person. You're the amazing one. I hope you know that." He hugged her then, and she hugged him back, holding him tightly as if she didn't want to let him go. When they pulled away, Kristen gave him a light kiss on the cheek, then turned and entered her house, closing the door softly behind her.

Later that evening, Ryan saw headlights out his front window and looked out to see who it was. There sat the BMW in front of Kristen's house, and Bradley was walking up her sidewalk.

Ryan sighed and turned away. Dr. BMW finally came after all the sad work was done. Ryan wished he were the one going over to Kristen's to comfort her. But at least he'd been there for her today, when she needed him most. Still, his heart ached at seeing Bradley there.

* * *

Bradley gave Kristen a quick hug and kiss on the cheek when she opened the door.

"Tough day?" he asked as they walked to the living room sofa and sat.

"Very tough."

"I'm sorry about your young friend," Bradley said softly. "This is why I've warned you so often not to become attached to your patients. It's difficult when they die. We're professionals, Kristen. Caring for the sick is our job, so in order to stay focused on what we need to do, we can't let our hearts become involved."

"Maybe that's easier for doctors and surgeons like yourself," Kristen said. "But for people like me who care for the daily needs of the patients, it's more difficult. We get to know them personally. We can't help but let our emotions become involved at times."

Bradley gave her an understanding smile. "I know, dear. And I realize it makes me sound cold-hearted when I talk this way. Believe me, I've lost patients and it hurts. That's why I distance myself from them personally. They are just cases to me. I know how harsh that sounds, but it's a way to protect myself from emotion so I can do the best job possible."

"I understand, and I know you're a good surgeon and you help people greatly. This case was different, though. Gabbie was different."

Bradley nodded, but Kristen knew he really didn't understand. They were two different people with different approaches about their profession. That, among so many other things, had helped her come to her decision.

"I called you to come over tonight to give you this back," Kristen said, handing him the velvet box that held her engagement ring. "I can't marry you, Bradley. I'm sorry."

Bradley sat up straighter. "Kristen. You can't mean that."

"Yes, I do. I've spent a lot of time thinking about us and I've realized our differences are too many to be married. I am honored that a man like you would want to marry me, but I can't."

"Kristen, you've had a stressful couple of days. This isn't the best time for you to make a big decision." He tried handing her the box back. "Think about it a little longer. I'm sure when you're feeling better, you'll change your mind."

Kristen shook her head and stood, walking to the living room window. She turned and faced Bradley. "No, I won't change my mind. I've given this considerable thought over the past two months. It just won't work. I love my home here and you live in the city. I love animals and want a dog, and I could tell you weren't thrilled with that idea. And most of all, I'm still holding out hope to have children someday. Your life is settled, and children would never fit into it."

Bradley looked as if he'd protest each item until she'd said children. Now, he just sat there, thoughtful. "I hadn't thought about you wanting children. I guess I assumed you were happy with just your work. You're right, at this stage in my life, I don't want to have children." He stood and walked over to where she was. "Are you sure, Kristen? We could have such a good life together. We have such a great companionship together."

"But that's the most important thing of all, Bradley. We're not in love with each other. You've never once told me that you love me. And I haven't said it to you, either. Shouldn't we both want more than just companionship?"

"Companionship can turn into affection. Even love."

"But I want love first."

"I understand," Bradley finally said. He walked back to the sofa and pocketed the ring, then headed to the entryway. Kristen followed him.

"I wish you only the best," he said, reaching out and giving her a hug. "I do care about you, Kristen. I wish we could have so much more."

"Goodbye, Bradley," she said softly. He gave her a small smile, then headed out the door.

After he left, Kristen didn't feel the loss she thought she would. She felt lighter. She could breathe easier now, no longer worrying if she should or shouldn't marry Bradley. He'd been right that it had been a stressful couple of days for her. But even if Gabbie hadn't died, she would have eventually said no to Bradley's proposal. She knew deep in her heart that they weren't right for each other. That she wanted more. Ryan had taught her that. She couldn't have lived with just a strong affection for the man she married—she needed passion. She wanted someone who desired her, cared about her, and wanted to be there for her. Emotionally and physically. All the things that came from falling in love with someone.

Keep him. Kristen heard Gabbie's soft voice echo in her ear.

"He's not mine to keep," she said aloud. Then she headed upstairs. She had a long week of work ahead of her.

* * *

The weeks slipped by and August came, bringing with it the heat and humidity that was normal for this time of year. Ryan had returned to his usual routine of working out in the company's gym each evening before heading home. Sometimes Jon was there, strolling on the treadmill beside him, talking more than exercising. Ryan didn't mind. Jon was more careful now how he referred to women since that night at Ryan's house. Ryan appreciated that. He'd always hated the crude way Jon talked about women.

Since Gabbie's funeral, Ryan had seen very little of Kristen. He'd invited her on walks on the weekends, but each time she already had plans. He supposed she was busy seeing Dr. BMW and planning her wedding. It still got under his skin that she was going to marry Bradley. The man didn't deserve her. And Ryan was going to miss her once they were married and she moved away. Sam would miss her, too. All Ryan could do was hope that she'd be happy.

On a Friday night after his workout, Ryan was in the locker room changing when Jon walked by dressed up for a night out.

"I don't suppose you'd like to join me for a beer tonight," Jon said.

Ryan didn't say no immediately as he usually did. He couldn't stand the idea of spending another weekend alone. Maybe there was a woman out there for him, somewhere. He couldn't have Kristen, so maybe it was time to accept that and meet new people.

"Sure. Why not? It might be fun," Ryan said.

Jon's face lit up. "Great! I know this nice quiet bar where the women are a little more mature and the music is more our style. No more chasing younger women for me. I've learned my lesson."

When they entered the bar, Ryan tried not to laugh out loud. Apparently, Jon's idea of older women were women in the twenty-five-to-thirty range. But it was nice being out again and the music was more subdued, so he didn't have to scream to be heard.

The place was crowded so they sat at the bar. Soft rock music drifted from the back corner of the room where a three-piece band was set up.

No sooner had they ordered their first beer than two women

came up to say hello to Jon. He quickly introduced them to Ryan, then disappeared onto the dance floor with one of the women. After a few minutes of awkward conversation, the other woman drifted off, which was a relief to Ryan. She was a little too spacey for him. He liked someone who could hold her own in an intelligent conversation, and that hadn't been her strong suit.

"Hey, handsome. What are you doing here?"

A voice spoke up beside Ryan and he turned to see a familiar face. "Nichole. I could ask you the same question. Isn't this place a little too tame for you?"

Nichole laughed and sat down beside him. "I like variety. But why are you here? I thought you were done with the bar scene."

Ryan shrugged. "I thought I'd give it another try. Sitting home alone isn't all it's cracked up to be, either."

Nichole stared at him curiously. "Alone? That's strange. I thought you and your neighbor had something going on."

"Neighbor? You mean Kristen? Oh, no, there's nothing going on there. We're just friends. In fact, she's engaged to a rich doctor."

"Hmm. I could have sworn that night she came over crying that you two had something going on."

Ryan shook his head. "No, she was just upset. Kristen's a nurse. She works with children cancer patients and one of her patients I met recently died. It was all very sad."

"I remember you telling me that. But then why did she come running to you instead of to her fiancé? I think there's more going on than you're admitting to yourself."

This made Ryan pause. He'd never thought about it before. Why hadn't she gone to Bradley instead? Bradley hadn't even come to the funeral. It had seemed like the most natural thing in the world for Kristen to come to him that night so he never questioned it.

"I'm not sure why she came to me first, but believe me, there is nothing going on between Kristen and me."

Nichole grinned at him. "Boy, are you wrong about that. Believe me, Ryan. Women don't run to just anyone when they're upset and crying their eyes out. If you were the first person she thought of to run to, it's because she trusts you. Obviously more than she does her fiancé. She has a thing for you, bud. And you may be a little slow on the uptake, but you have a thing for her, too. I saw how upset you were over her crying. You have it bad. So, let me ask you again. What are you doing *here*?"

Ryan frowned. He thought about that night and how Kristen had come running to him, falling to pieces. Nichole was right. Women don't run next door to just anyone if they're upset, unless they trust the person they're going to. Kristen had trusted him with her feelings and run to him at a vulnerable time. She'd let him care for her, and had even asked him to stay with her that night. At the time, he'd just been happy to be able to care for her. Now, he wondered why she hadn't wanted Bradley with her instead?

She wanted you, you idiot. You.

Ryan looked up at Nichole. "You're right. I do have feelings for Kristen. I've been pushing them aside because I didn't feel I had a right to tell her. What an idiot I am. I need to go tell her how I feel. She needs to know before she makes the biggest mistake of her life."

Excited now, Ryan stood up. He reached out and hugged Nichole. "Thank you. Whatever happens tonight, at least I'll know I tried."

Nichole grinned. "What are you waiting for? Get out of here."

Ryan smiled wide, kissed her on the cheek, and headed for the exit. He caught Jon's eye across the room and waved so he'd know he was leaving. Then he went outside and walked quickly to his car, all the while forming in his head what he wanted to say to Kristen.

* * *

Kristen came home from work and went through her usual routine. She changed into jeans and a sweatshirt, and then heated up a pan of chicken noodle soup. Pulling a loaf of French bread out of the cupboard, she stood at the counter, slicing it. It was almost six o'clock and she noticed that Ryan's car wasn't in the driveway yet.

"He's probably out with some cute girl. It is Friday, after all," she said to the empty room. Kristen looked around. She'd been talking to empty rooms a lot lately. But it was her own fault. She could have gone out with the other nurses on her shift after work, but she'd declined. She could have called her sister to go to dinner with, but she hadn't. "You're alone because you choose to be," she said.

Kristen finished slicing the bread, put it on a plate, and covered it with a towel to heat up when the soup was ready. She went outside and stood on the stoop, inhaling the summer air. The sun wouldn't go down for a couple of hours, and she thought that she should have walked with Sam before making dinner. She was just so tired after her workweek that she didn't have the energy tonight.

She was just about to go inside when she caught sight of Sam coming out her doggie door. Sam walked to the gate and stared at Kristen, smiling and wagging her tail.

Kristen wondered if Sam was lonely too, waiting for Ryan to come home. *Hmm. Maybe we could keep each other company.*

Smiling to herself, Kristen ran inside and wrote a note for Ryan. "*Sam's with me. Come get her when you get home.*" She went outside again and taped it to his kitchen door, then opened the back gate and let Sam out.

"Want to come to my house for a while?" she asked Sam.

Kristen didn't have to ask twice. Sam happily followed her home.

Kristen found a can of dog food left over from the last time she'd cared for Sam and put it in a bowl for her. Then she ladled soup into a bowl for and heated up the bread in the microwave. Kristen sat down at the kitchen table and ate her dinner while Sam ate hers.

"Now I don't have to talk to myself," Kristen said, patting Sam on the head. "Do you want to hear about my day?"

Sam didn't object so Kristen started talking.

* * *

Ryan tried not to rush as he drove home, but it was difficult to keep his speed down. Friday night traffic leaving downtown was always crazy in the summer and all he wanted was to get to Kristen's before it was too late to knock on her door.

It was a quarter to nine when he pulled into his driveway and he was happy to see that Kristen's car was in hers and the BMW wasn't parked on the street. He jumped out of the car and didn't even bother to put his briefcase in the house. He wanted to see Kristen.

When he got to her kitchen door, however, he hesitated. *What if she isn't at all interested in me? What if she thinks I'm crazy?* Ryan took a deep breath to steel himself, then knocked on her door.

A dog barked at his knock and Ryan wondered why. Did Kristen get a dog? He knocked again, louder this time, and waited. Finally, Kristen opened the door looking sleepy.

"Oh, no. I woke you up," he said, suddenly feeling stupid for banging on her door. He was surprised to see Sam standing there beside her, wagging her tail.

"No, it's fine," Kristen said, yawning. "I must have fallen asleep watching a movie. I see you got my note."

"Note? What note?"

"The one I left on your door telling you I had Sam. Sorry I stole your dog. I just wanted company and I could tell you weren't home yet."

"Oh. No. That's fine. You can steal Sam anytime."

Kristen looked at him curiously. "If you didn't see my note, why did you stop by?"

Ryan wavered. Should he tell her? Was he crazy to tell her he was falling in love with her? Finally, he asked, "Can I come in?"

"Sure. Sorry. I should have asked you to come in. Come on."

Ryan walked inside and Kristen closed the door.

"I went out with Jon tonight to grab a beer and I ran into Nichole. She made me realize something that I should have known all along. That's why I'm here."

Kristen's eyes dropped. "Oh. That you're in love with her?"

"No. Not with her. I'm in love with you."

Kristen's eyes flew up to his. "Me?"

Ryan took a step closer to Kristen. "Yes. You. Kristen, I've had feelings for you for some time now. Why do you think I kissed you both times? I couldn't help it. I'm drawn to you. I tried not pressing you because I knew you were engaged to Bradley, but I can't let you marry him without at least telling you how I feel. I love you, Kristen."

Kristen's eyes filled with tears. "Me? Really?"

Ryan smiled down at her. "Yes, you. Really. I haven't felt this way about anyone since Amanda. You're sweet and caring and you have a big heart. And you're beautiful. I love your gorgeous eyes, your hair, your smile. I love everything about you. I can't think of anyone else I'd rather spend the day with, walk in the park with, or even go furniture shopping with. Just you. There's no one else I'd rather fall asleep with at night and wake up in the morning with except you."

"Oh, Ryan. I don't know what to say."

Ryan took another step closer and lightly placed his hands on her arms. "Please say you feel the same way. Don't marry Bradley. He'll never love you the way I do. I promise I'll never do anything to hurt you. You can trust me to love you, and only you. Please, don't marry Bradley."

Kristen looked up into his eyes. "I'm not marrying Bradley. I broke it off with him weeks ago, after Gabbie's funeral. I knew he wasn't the right one for me."

Ryan's eyes grew wide. "You did? Why didn't you tell me? I thought you'd been avoiding me because you were with him."

"I needed time to sort out my life and my feelings, that's why I didn't tell you. I knew you had feelings for me. You told me you did the night of the fireworks. But I was still in denial. Now, I know what I want. Who I want."

"Who?"

Kristen smiled as tears spilled down her cheeks. "You, silly. I want you."

Ryan laughed and pulled her close. "I was so afraid you didn't want me. I love you, Kristen."

"I love you, too," Kristen said.

Ryan dropped his lips to hers.

Sam barked once and sat down close to them. Both Ryan and Kristen pulled away and smiled down at her.

"I love you, too, Sam," Kristen said, patting her head. "If it wasn't for you, we wouldn't have found each other."

Sam only grinned at her.

Epilogue

One Year Later

Kristen, Ryan, and Sam walked along the shore of Lake Harriet, enjoying the beautiful summer evening. The past year had been a whirlwind for them. After the night that Ryan had declared his love for Kristen, they'd spent every spare moment together. They took walks as often as they could, even in the winter. They enjoyed eating dinner together each night and invited Kristen's sister, Heather, and her boyfriend, Doug, over often. And two months after they'd become a couple, they flew to Cedar Rapids to visit Ryan's family as Ruth happily babysat the cats and Sam. Just as Marla had predicted, Kristen was perfect for Ryan and she fit easily into the family. Kristen adored Ryan's family. It was nice, after all these years of having only her sister, to finally have a family she could call her own.

On Valentine's Day, Ryan proposed, and Kristen accepted immediately. She didn't have to think about it with Ryan—she knew he was the man she'd been waiting for her entire life.

They married on a warm day in May beside the blue waters of Lake Harriet with family all around. Ryan's family had flown in from Iowa and filled Ryan's house and the guest cottage. Heather was Kristen's maid of honor, and Stacy's husband, Gerald, was the best man. James offered to walk Kristen down the aisle and her heart burst with happiness to have him as her father, too. After years of not trusting men, she now had so many good men around her she felt she could trust.

But most of all, she trusted Ryan with her heart, and she knew he wouldn't disappoint her.

And of course, Sam was in the wedding, sitting at attention beside the bride wearing a bow around her neck. Without Sam as their one connection, Kristen would never have gotten to know Ryan so well, and she held a special place in Kristen's heart.

They had a small reception in Ryan's backyard and Ruth came as did Jon and also Nichole. After hearing that it was Nichole who'd pointed out to Ryan that he was in love with Kristen, she invited her, now thinking of her as a friend. Kristen would be forever grateful to Nichole for sending Ryan to her.

The couple had moved into Ryan's house before the wedding and put Kristen's up for sale. They'd decided that his house had more room for guests, because of the cottage, and they hoped that now that Marla was feeling better, she and James would visit often. Marla had been declared cancer-free in March, and even though the family knew her chances of getting cancer again were high, they all hoped for the best. Marla and James could now enjoy their retirement, and they planned several trips over the next few years to make the most of it.

Kristen never once worried about the memory of Amanda in Ryan's house. In fact, as he was about to put away the last of the photos of his deceased wife, Kristen insisted they keep one out. Amanda had been a big part of his life, and Kristen wasn't jealous of her. She knew that Ryan loved her now, and there was space in the house for both of them.

Kristen had sold her house to a young couple and she and Ryan were thrilled to have young neighbors next door. The house deserved a young family and Ryan and Kristen hoped the couple would stay for years to come.

And now, three months after they'd been married, Ryan and Kristen strolled through the park with Sam. Kristen placed her hand over her stomach and smiled. It wouldn't be just the three of them for long. She was three months pregnant, and they were both excited to be expecting their first child.

"Ready to go home?" Ryan asked Kristen as he smiled down at her.

Kristen nodded. She took ahold of Sam's leash and the three of them headed home.

###

About the Author

Deanna Lynn Sletten grew up in southern California before moving to northern Minnesota as a teenager. Her interest in writing novels was sparked in a college English class and she has been writing in some form or another ever since. In 2011, Deanna discovered the world of self-publishing and published three novels she'd written over the years. After that, she was hooked. Deanna has written eleven novels and is currently working on her next novel due to be published by Lake Union Publishing in 2016.

Deanna enjoys writing heartwarming women's fiction and romance novels with unforgettable characters. She has also written one middle-grade novel that takes you on the adventure of a lifetime. She believes in fate, destiny, love at first sight, soul mates, second chances, and happily ever after, and her novels reflect that.

Deanna is married and has two grown children. When not writing, she enjoys walking the wooded trails around her home with her beautiful Australian Shepherd or relaxing in the boat on the lake in the summer.

Deanna loves hearing from her readers. Connect with her at:
Her blog: www.deannalynnsletten.com/
Facebook: www.facebook.com/DeannaLynnSletten
Twitter: @DeannaLSletten
Find more novels by Deanna Lynn Sletten at her Amazon Author Page

Made in United States
Troutdale, OR
08/02/2023

11751060R00116